Her lips were pink and soft and wet . . .

and, as he looked down at them, so inviting. He gazed into her eyes, those eyes that watched him, read him. He wondered if she saw everything.

"Well . . . good night," she whispered.

"Wait."

She didn't turn away, didn't back down, as he came as close as he could without touching her. He told himself to stop it now, that there was too much at stake, that if he let this happen again, there would be no more controlling his feelings.

"I want to kiss you," he said.

She felt his breath on her lips, and wet them again. "That's not a good idea."

"No," he said. "It isn't, is it?"

They looked at each other for what seemed a fragment of eternity. Then he lowered his face and his lips grazed hers, and before taking her completely, he whispered, "But I'm gonna do it anyway."

ABOUT THE AUTHOR

Tracy Hughes began writing her first romance
novel after graduating from Northeast Louisiana
University in 1984. While in graduate school, she
finished that book in lieu of her thesis, and
decided to abandon her pursuit of a master's
degree and follow her dream of becoming a
writer. She is the award-winning author of
nineteen novels, including a mainstream and a
historical romance. Tracy recently relocated to
Mississippi, where she makes her home with her
two young daughters.

Books by Tracy Hughes

HARLEQUIN AMERICAN ROMANCE

381–HONORBOUND

HARLEQUIN SUPERROMANCE

304–ABOVE THE CLOUDS
342–JO: CALLOWAY CORNERS, BOOK 2
381–EMERALD WINDOWS
399–WHITE LIES AND ALIBIS

Don't miss any of our special offers. Write to us at the
following address for information on our newest releases.

Harlequin Reader Service
P.O. Box 1397, Buffalo, NY 14240
Canadian address: P.O. Box 603,
Fort Erie, Ont. L2A 5X3

TRACY HUGHES

SECOND CHANCES

Harlequin Books

TORONTO • NEW YORK • LONDON
AMSTERDAM • PARIS • SYDNEY • HAMBURG
STOCKHOLM • ATHENS • TOKYO • MILAN

Published October 1991

ISBN 0-373-16410-6

SECOND CHANCES

Chapter One

Cassandra's life is worth two million dollars, to be delivered tonight. If you ever want to see her alive again, do not involve police and answer on first ring.

Leah Borgadeux wadded the damp, typewritten note in her trembling hand and bit her lip. She'd read it a thousand times since Casey had been snatched from her baby-sitter's yard over four hours ago, but each time she read it, her terror only heightened.

The noise of electronic equipment being set up in the corner of her small kitchen punctuated the cold reality of the nightmare that had her in its grip.

She stroked the threadbare baby blanket draped over her arm and hugged Casey's sticky old Bunny Fu-Fu to her chest. She closed her eyes and tried not to think about how lost the two-year-old would be tonight without these favorite items.

"Why don't they call?" she asked rhetorically, her voice hoarse from hours of near hysteria. "They said in the ransom note they would call."

"Pull yourself together," Lance Borgadeux said as he paced across the room, his large, intimidating frame dwarfing the tiny beach house. "They'll call."

She gave her father a cursory glance and remembered vividly why she had moved out from under his thumb before Casey was born, despite the fact that, ever since, he'd tried to paint Leah as insecure and irresponsible. The kidnapping was just one more piece of data in his "can't-take-care-of-herself" file.

"Of course they'll call," she echoed sarcastically. "They would never break their word to an almighty Borgadeux. Just because they snatched a two-year-old asthmatic baby from her sitter and left a two-million-dollar ransom note doesn't mean they'd break their word!"

"Calm down," her father replied. "They want the money. They'll call, damn it!" He turned back to one of the detectives. "Call a doctor. Get Leah a tranquilizer or something."

"I don't *need* a tranquilizer!" she shouted. "I need my baby! She's out there with God-knows-who—"

Her father caught her arms and shook her. "You're falling apart, Leah! You've got to stop this."

Leah pivoted out of his arms and shook her head. "No tranquilizers, Dad. Just make them find Casey."

"They will."

He came up behind her, turned her back around and pulled her into that rough, demanding hug that had been the benchmark of her security for most of her

life. Long ago, she had stopped wondering if a
mother's embrace would have been softer, more
tender. Her mother had died in childbirth with Leah,
leaving Leah with only the real-estate tycoon to parent her, and no basis for comparison. Until three years
ago it had been enough.

But Leah hadn't known better then.

Slipping out of his arms, she walked to the open
glass doors and out onto the deck that overlooked the
Gulf, and tried to concentrate on the surf pounding
against the shore. The ocean breeze whispered through
her soft blond hair—hair that seemed so compatible
with the sun and sea—but she couldn't feel the peace
nor the healing that it usually offered.

"Maybe we can catch 'em before you 'ave to let go
of the money." She looked over her shoulder to the
three detectives her father had brought here with him.
The one with the plaid tie and the Australian accent
addressed her father instead of her. "We 'ave people
working on it in the field right now."

Leah turned around and clutched the blanket and
bunny tighter to her chest. "I don't care about the
money," she said. "I don't want some idiot I don't
even know jeopardizing my daughter's life. They said
they'd kill her if they thought we'd gone to the police."

As if this was just another corporate game that
wasn't going to ruffle him, Borgadeux put his arm
around Leah's shoulder and escorted her back to the
open doors. "No one's jeopardizing Cassandra's life,
honey," he said in a quiet, condescending voice.
"These are pros. I've used them over and over in my

own business, and they're very discreet. The kidnappers will never know. But if you want to get Cassandra back, sweetheart, you'll have to cooperate with them."

"Her name's Casey," Leah corrected, though she knew it hardly mattered now. "I call her Casey, Daddy. Why won't you ever call her Casey?"

"Because it's a stupid name," he said. "Cassandra is a beautiful name for a beautiful little girl."

"You never give up," she said under her breath, a hopeless note of despair flattening her tone.

She moved away from him, stepped farther out onto the balcony and felt the cool wind blustering against her house. Yesterday it had been ninety-three degrees, not unusual for October in Florida. But today a cold front had moved in and the temperature had dropped to the seventies.

As always, with abrupt weather changes, Casey had awakened that morning congested and wheezing. Her theophylline, Ventolin and nebulizer treatments had stabilized her enough that Leah had felt safe keeping an appointment that afternoon. But once the medicine began to wear off around three, Casey was sure to have trouble breathing again. It was now five o'clock, and the thought of the little girl crying, coughing and wheezing was more than she could stand.

"She needs her medicine," she said aloud for the thousandth time that day. "What if she gets really sick, and they panic and—"

"They won't. They'll call any minute now, we'll make the switch and you'll have Casey back."

"Right." The hopeless word matched the look of doubt in her blue eyes as she gazed out over the Gulf. In the distance, the horizon was blurred with black clouds moving across the water. There was going to be a storm.

Already, it looked violent. Coastal storms always were. Lightning would perform its lethal show across the sky, the earth would shake, the sky would grumble. Electricity would flicker and, perhaps, go out altogether. And Casey would scream.

She brought the blanket to her eyes and tried to squeeze back the tears. It still smelled of the little toddler—baby powder, Tootsie Pops and Kool-Aid. She wished she'd followed the doctor's advice and broken Casey of that last bottle of the day months ago. At least that would be one less thing she'd expect....

The thought of her baby's state of mind, now that she'd been in a stranger's hands for much of the day, made Leah's stomach knot and sink with nausea. Why didn't they call? Why couldn't they just tell her where to take the money and get it over with?

Ben, the detective who seemed in charge, stepped out onto the balcony and handed her a cordless phone. "They said t'answer on the first ring," he said, his soft accent momentarily distracting her from her terror. "Don't worry about us. Our equipment is all set t'start tracing the minute you answer. You'll want t' keep 'im on as long as you can. Tell 'im about the asthma and the medication she needs. Just keep 'im on."

She looked down at the phone, vaguely aware that her palm was sweating, making it difficult to hold. "Yes. All right."

He went to the railing of the deck, sat down and pulled a pencil out of his pocket. Flipping open his notepad, he made a notation, then glanced out over the water. "Storm's comin'. Hope it don't interfere with the telephone lines."

She swallowed and looked out toward the clouds again.

"Prob'ly won't," he added. "Listen, if you're up to it, I need t'ask a few more questions."

"Yes," she said. "Anything."

"Well we've already got people checking out everyone Casey sees from day to day, but I need ya t' rack your brain once more. Is there anyone you may 'ave left out? I know she's only two, but does she 'ave any friends she plays with on a regular basis? Any preschool teachers? Church nursery workers? Ballet instructors? Anyone who knows she's Lance Borgadeux's granddaughter and saw a quick buck to be made?"

Leah sat down on a patio chair and tried to steady her trembling hands. "I've already told you everyone I can think of. Since I left home and moved here, I haven't had a very high standard of living. Nothing to indicate my father's wealth. I don't think anyone here knows anything about the Borgadeux."

"Everybody knows about the Borgadeux," her father said, the pronouncement an aggravating combination of pride and long-suffering chagrin. "Everybody's suspect. Especially those who pretended not to know or care."

Frustrated, Ben jotted a few comments and shook his head. He seemed to hesitate on the next question, and he shot Borgadeux a tentative look. "Mr. Borgadeux, I know this next question won't meet with your approval—"

"Then don't ask it."

Leah snapped a look at her father. "What question?"

"I *'ave* t'ask," Ben said, still addressing her father. "If I didn't, I'd be overlooking a vital area that could 'elp us crack this—"

"What vital area?" She turned from her father to Ben, appalled. "This is *my* child we're talking about. *Mine*. If you have something to ask me, you ask it. And, Daddy, you have no right to stop him!"

"He wants to ask about the child's father, Leah!" her father bellowed. "I told him to leave him out of this—"

She swung back to the detective. "Her father didn't have anything to do with this, but damn it, *my* father had no right to stop you from asking."

She walked to the edge of the deck, trying to steady her breathing, and told herself that her father's manipulation was nothing new. He had successfully convinced her to walk out on Jeff over two and a half years ago, and she hadn't forgiven him for it yet. Now he thought he could manipulate the factors of the investigation just as he'd always manipulated the factors of her life.

The sky grew darker, and a few drops of rain began to fall. She made no move to go in. "Casey's father's name is Jeff Hampton. He lives in Tampa."

Ben scribbled the name on his pad. "Miss Borgadeux, I know this is painful for you, but we have t' know more about 'er father. In the case of two parents living apart, it's not unusual for a kidnapping t'occur.''

Leah twirled one of the bunny's ears around her finger and drew her brows together in a frown that bore more remorse than she'd ever known what to do with. "It would be unusual in this case," she said quietly. "He doesn't even know Casey exists. And I prefer to keep it that way."

Ben intercepted Borgadeux's I-told-you-so look and rose to face her. "Look, Miss Borgadeux, I understand your desire for discretion, for whatever reason, but suppose...just suppose...that the father discovered 'e 'as a child and decided to get revenge for your keeping it a secret. We 'ave to at least consider that possibility."

"Jeff isn't vindictive like that," she whispered. "He would never do anything like this."

"But 'e could 'ave found out. Dunedin isn't more than twenty minutes from Tampa. He could have seen you with Casey, or heard about her from a mutual friend. He could have—"

"He would have confronted me if he heard," she said with certainty. "He would have come to me."

"People change. They get bitter. Angry. Sometimes they don't react to things the way we think they will."

Leah wiped a stray tear off her face with the blanket, and tried to sort out the rhymes and reasons in her head. A drop of rain fell onto the ribbon edging the quilting, drawing her attention to a stain there. She wondered where it had come from. Had Casey dragged the blanket through the dirt at the park again?

"She said to leave him out of it," Borgadeux said, his powerful voice quieting the detective. "He doesn't have anything to do with this. He's gone this long without knowing about Cassandra. Just because she was kidnapped is no reason to drag him into it now."

The rain began to drizzle harder, but Leah still made no attempt to go inside. Neither Borgadeux nor Ben made a move to leave the deck, either.

"He'll find out now anyway, y'know," the detective pointed out. "When this is all over, regardless of the turnout, it'll be all over the media. Whether he was involved in it or not, he'll know then."

"He won't know Casey's his," Borgadeux said.

Leah snapped her gaze to her father, astounded. "Yes, he will. I wasn't sleeping around, Daddy. I was in love with him. I would have married him—" Her voice cracked midsentence, and she turned away.

The rain was falling harder now, and she could see the lightning moving closer. In moments they would hear its thunder and feel its wrath on her home. As much as she wanted to stand out here and let the cool rain wash away her mistakes and regrets, as much as she wanted to defy the sky and dare the lightning, she couldn't.

That would be as foolhardy, as devastating, as bringing Jeff in on this now.

She heard the door slide open, and her father tapped her arm. "We'll talk about it inside," he said.

"You and Ben go on in," she said. "I'll be right there."

"Don't wait too long, honey. The storm's getting ugly."

She nodded and watched the power of the lightning, still miles away on the water. It wouldn't take long to reach her. It never did.

It had been raining and thundering the day she'd left him, and now, as a fissure of lightning split the sky in the distance, she recalled when she'd told him it was over. His wet black hair had waved and slapped against his head, as if demonstrating the pain and anger she had seen in the obsidian depths of his eyes. And he'd had a right to be angry. Anyone would.

"You love me," he had pleaded, as though reminding her could wipe away the inevitable heartache she seemed so bent on inflicting. "I know you love me."

She had wanted to fall into his arms and scream yes, that she loved him. But her love was a weapon...a destroyer that brought ruin to those who had the misfortune of loving her back.

Images of her mother's face had danced like a phantom across her heart. The face had been an image she had only seen in photographs since Leah had never known her mother. Images of the dog she had loved, the dog who had gotten too rough in their play and had bitten her. Her father had gotten rid of it that very afternoon. Images of the nanny she had loved, the only woman who had molded her and cared for her and influenced her—too much, according to her father, who had fired her and refused to give references to account for the four years she had devoted to Leah.

Everyone who had ever loved her had met with misfortune…and regardless of how her father's hand had always helped it along, the threat remained real.

And then her father had handed down one of his famous ultimatums, at a time when Jeff was on the threshold of taking his contracting business from breaking even to breaking records. The contract on the Suncoast Dome in St. Petersburg had been all but his after years of hard work, but her father had the contacts and the means to destroy that dream, ruin his reputation and break the man.

Unless she refused to marry him and never saw him again.

Those were the things playing through her mind that day she had left him. So she had carried out the charade of fickle rich girl who didn't care about him anymore, and had aptly convinced him that it was over.

But neither of them had known then that she was pregnant.

Weeks later, when she learned that she was carrying his child, she had searched her soul and found that she didn't have the strength to keep this secret from him. Wouldn't a baby fill the void that a foiled business would cause? Together, couldn't they weather that storm? Wasn't this baby worth any fight?

But the questions had never been answered, for Jeff, so steeply entrenched in bitterness and hatred for her, had refused to take her repeated calls. When she'd tried to see him, he'd slammed the door in her face. Letters she'd sent had come back unopened.

Finally, she had accepted that the baby was hers alone, and she had moved away from her father's estate, determined not to let him force any more ultimatums on her. She had hoped to never need him again.

But she'd never counted on Casey being kidnapped.

Somehow, that changed things. She needed for Jeff to know about Casey. She needed to be purged of that sin for which she was certain she was being punished.

She went back inside, realizing only now that she was soaked clear through to her skin. A shiver coursed through her.

"I'll do whatever it takes to get Casey back," she told Ben. "And if you think contacting her father will help, then I'll go along with it."

"But, Leah! You're opening a Pandora's box. You'll regret it!"

She didn't look at her father as Ben shoved the notebook into his coat pocket. "Willy and I'll go question 'im now, and Jack can stay in case we 'ear from the kidnappers. We'll have t' take your Jaguar, Mr. Borgadeux, since we didn't come in our own car. If the 'ouse is being watched, they'll just think one of you is leaving. They won't see us through the tinted windows."

"Wait."

Ben turned back to her, and she saw relief draining the tension from her father's face. He thought she was going to back down, she mused.

New tears pushed to blur her vision as she stepped toward the detective. "Could you... could you question him without telling him everything? I mean... could you let me...?"

"Let you what?" the confused detective asked. "Question 'im?"

"No," she said, her voice wobbling. "Let me tell him who Casey is. I want to be the one to tell him."

"Honey, don't do that to yourself," Lance said, coming to her side. "If they have to question him, let them do it and be done with it. It's none of his business."

"None of his business?" she asked her father, half laughing in disbelief. "He's her father. I don't think for a minute he could have taken her. But if he did find out, he'd have every right to want revenge. Besides..." Her voice trailed off, and she felt that defeated horror wash over her again. "I need to see him. I *need* to tell him. I've waited too long already."

"But he'll hurt you again. Just like the last time."

Leah looked fully at her father for the first time since he'd walked in here today with a briefcase full of money. And all the old anger came rushing back to remind her why she'd left home in the first place. "He didn't hurt me, Daddy. I hurt him, remember?"

And there was nothing Lance Borgadeux could say. For he remembered it well.

THE MEMORIES CAME RUSHING back to Jeff with confusing clarity the moment the gold Jaguar with plates bearing the name *Borgy 1* drove up to the trailer on the work site where he kept his office. From the scaffold on the fourth-floor level of what was to be the new home of the Sunshine Bank, he watched two men get out, look around, then start inside the trailer.

They were looking for him. He knew it instinctively, for he had never forgotten the way Borgy's "people" had tailed and harassed and bribed him before, when he'd been determined to marry Leah. But that was all history, and they had gotten what they wanted. He couldn't imagine what they wanted with him now.

Not anxious to find out, he stayed where he was. If they were to meet their deadline on this building, he couldn't lose one man-hour right now. Even if it was his own. They had all committed to working every daylight hour to complete the job, and from the looks of the sky, a storm would break soon, forcing them to quit for the day, anyway. Until it reached them, they had to move forward. That dedication to finishing the job was why he was so successful. He had the best crew in Tampa Bay, and he was a hands-on builder who saw his projects through to the very end. It might not look so good to a man who wanted only "the best" husband for his daughter...someone who spent his days philosophizing in an executive think tank, and drove a Jaguar with eighteen-carat gold trim...but it was what Jeff had chosen to do. It was good that he liked it, he mused cynically, because for the last two and a half years, it was all he'd had.

He glanced back toward the car and decided to let Jan handle them. He'd lost enough time on Borgadeux, he thought. The last thing he needed was to dredge up those old, buried memories again.

Bending down on one knee, he checked the bolts on the steel frame, and put the car and its passengers out of his mind. Jeff concentrated on wrapping his work up before the storm hit.

INSIDE THE TRAILER, Jeff's sister and secretary, Jan Hampton, gave her best shot at questioning the two detectives before they could question her brother.

"Just tell me one thing and I'll show you where he is," the woman said, running long fingers through her short-cropped raven hair and assessing the Australian carefully. "Tell me what two detectives would have to question him about. He hasn't done anything wrong."

"Maybe 'e has, maybe 'e ain't," Ben countered. "No way to tell till we talk to 'im."

"Where are you from?" Jan asked. "England?"

Ben snickered. "No, I ain't from bloody England. I 'ail from Australia. Now are you gonna show us where we can find 'im, or do we 'ave to—"

"Australia." Jan leaned back against her desk and crossed her arms. "How do I know I can trust some foreigner carrying a gun?"

"I ain't carryin' a gun, lady," Ben said.

"But he is," she said, undauntedly opening the coat of the man standing beside him. Willy slapped his hand over his pistol and straightened his jacket, indignant.

"I'll ask again. How can I trust a couple of pistol-packing foreigners looking for my brother?"

"Damn it, we'll find 'im ourselves," Ben said, starting back for the door.

"Good luck," she said. "There are eighty other men out there. And they get real quiet when strangers start asking questions."

Ben threw a look back over his shoulder to Willy. "Go back to the car, Willy, and radio for reinforcements. We're going to 'ave to use force, I guess."

Jan's eyebrows shot up. "Reinforcements? That won't be necessary." She pointed out the window. "He's up there, on the scaffold. Geez, you people. A girl tries to protect her brother from a couple of Dick Tracy clones, and you start threatening her."

The two detectives opened the door and started out, and Jan followed close on their heels. "Hey, you guys aren't gonna arrest him or anything without telling him what he did, are you? You can't do that, can you?"

Without answering, the detectives started toward the scaffold.

IT WAS JUST STARTING to drizzle when Jeff saw the two men coming toward him, and heaving a sigh and wondering what the hell was up, he made his way down and started toward them.

Jan trailed behind them, a look of distress on her face, but that was nothing unusual, he mused. Her feathers were always ruffled about something. The detectives wore a look of dead seriousness, and Jeff couldn't imagine why they'd be looking for him on old Borgy's behalf. Jeff had done what Borgadeux had wanted and let his daughter go over two and a half years ago. What else did the man want?

"You looking for me?" Jeff asked as he reached the men.

"They threatened me," Jan cut in. "One of them's carrying a gun."

Jeff gave them a slight frown, then glanced over his shoulder to see if any of his crew around him had heard. None seemed particularly interested in the conversation, for most were hurrying to reach stopping points before the sky opened up. "What's going on?" he asked in a quieter voice.

Again, Jan piped in before Ben could answer. "They're detectives, Jeff."

"Detectives?" He started to laugh, and shaking his head, pushed past them into the trailer. The men followed him.

"That's great," he said. "Detectives. Again. Isn't the jerk satisfied that I don't want anything of his? What kind of dirt is he looking for this time?"

Ben gave Willy a confused look, then took out his ID and flashed it. "Look, mate, I don't know what the 'ell you're talkin' about, but we're 'ere to question you about your whereabouts earlier today."

Jeff walked to the sink, set his hard hat on the rim, and began washing his hands. "That's easy. I've been here all day."

"Can you confirm that?" Ben asked.

"*I* can," Jan interjected. "He's been here since seven this morning and hasn't left all day."

"Anybody else around who can confirm it, mate?" Ben asked, ignoring her. "No offense, lady, but you ain't what I call a credible witness."

Jan started to object, but Jeff stopped her. "Help yourself," he said, drying his hands. "There's a whole team of guys out there who can vouch for me. I haven't left here all day."

"Guess 'e's clean, then," Ben said, glancing at his cohort with disappointment. "Willy, go on out and confirm 'is alibi."

The quieter detective started out of the trailer, and Ben looked at the scuffed floor and cleared his throat. "Uh, I'm sorry, mate, but I need you to come with me for an hour or so. Won't take long, but my orders are to bring you in for some...er...some questioning."

"About what? And what do you mean, check out my alibi? What do I need an alibi for?"

"I'll tell you when we get there. Come on now. It's easier if you come peaceful."

Jeff glanced at his sister. "Do you believe this guy?" He shook his head at the detective. "Tell old Borgy that he can't send his thugs out to pick me up at a whim. I'm not going."

"Then we'll have to take you by force. And all your crew 'll see their boss in 'andcuffs at gunpoint. Wouldn't look too good, eh?"

"You've gotta be kidding."

"No, joke, mate. I don't want to do it that way. I'd rather you just come with us for an hour or so, and we'll bring you right back 'ere."

Jeff set his hands on his hips and stared at the man, realizing he was dead serious. Finally, he unhooked his tool belt and handed it to Jan. "All right, I'll go and get this damn thing over with. It's Borgadeux's car they came in," he said. "Maybe I'll get the chance to bash the jackass's face in."

"Borgadeux?" Jan asked, still holding the tool belt. "I can't believe this. Does it have anything to do with Leah? Because if it does, Jeff, I hope I don't have to remind you that she dumped you. You spent a year scraping yourself up off the ground after she trampled all over you."

"Don't worry. I'm immune. She's like a disease you only have once. It can't get you twice."

The rain began to come harder, pounding on the aluminum roof of the trailer. Slinging down the towel, he started to the door.

"Jeff, please be careful."

Jeff's sarcastic smile held no joy as he looked back over his shoulder. "With Borgy or Leah?"

"Leah," his sister said. "You can handle that slimeball father of hers. But she's charmed your pants off before."

"I told you. I'm immune. I'm not the same person."

"But she is," Jan said.

"That's just the thing," he said. "I never really knew who that was."

Jeff started out into the rain, now pounding hard on the dirt, and Ben followed him. Already the structure had cleared and his crew were dispersing and heading for the cars and trucks lined behind the trailer. Some of the men who Willy had approached were now standing near the car, watching with curiosity.

"Alibi checks out," Willy said, dashing through the rain to the back door of the car. He opened the door and took Jeff's arm to urge him in.

"Get your hands off me!" Jeff told him. "Touch me again and I'll break your neck."

"Sorry." Willy raised his hands innocently and went around the car to the passenger side as Jeff got in.

"Look, nobody wants to hurt you," the detective in the front said as he started the car. "You've got a solid alibi, so you obviously had nothin' t' do with the kidnappin'. We just 'ave to take you in to—"

"*Kidnapping?*" He leaned forward in the seat and glared at Ben. "What kidnapping?"

"Never mind, mate."

By the way the man had shut up, Jeff wondered if it had been a slip. Kidnapping. He sat back, frowning out the black-tinted window, and tried not to dwell on that word.

Was it Leah? Had someone abducted her?

An irrational, maddening, self-betraying fear skidded up inside him as images of terrorists, of murderers, of rapists holding her at their mercy flashed like freeze-frames in his mind. Could they appreciate more than the dollar signs that hovered over her like a man-made halo? Would they hurt her?

He cleared his throat, swallowed. "Look, pal. I have a right to know." His voice sounded foreign, hollow. "When was she kidnapped? Where was she?"

Via the rearview mirror, he saw the condemning look pass from the driver to Willy.

"Did we say it was a 'she?'" the Aussie asked. "I don't remember sayin', do you, Willy?"

"Nope. Neither of us said."

"Give me a break." Jeff bracketed his hands over the seat in front of him and leaned forward again. "You questioned *me* about it. You picked me up in one of the Borgadeux chariots. You tell me someone's been kidnapped. Who the hell else could it be but Leah?"

"Try Cassandra, mate," the driver said. "Cassandra Borgadeux."

A flood of relief washed over Jeff as he sat back in his seat. Cassandra. Not Leah. He didn't know a Cassandra Borgadeux. Probably a cousin or aunt or something, he thought. But not Leah.

He stroked his lip with his rough, tanned index finger, and for the first time noted beads of sweat there, despite the air conditioning that filled the car. Damn it, why had he let the thought of Leah in danger shake him that way? She had chosen to lead the life of the pampered heiress, and had discarded him like trash.

He could never forget that.

They reached the Courtney Campbell Causeway that would take them from Tampa into Clearwater, and over the bay he saw darker clouds billowing in angry orchestration. Bolts of lightning cracked across the sky, and thunder shook the earth. There had been a storm the day she'd left him, he recalled. A storm much like this one, brilliant and magnificent in its force and power, but that brilliance could also be deadly and devastating.

His heart twisted at the bittersweet memory of the woman who had pierced his heart over two and a half years ago, and he wondered if he was about to see her. God, he hoped not. The last thing he needed in his life right now was Leah Borgadeux bringing him to his knees again.

So a Borgadeux had been kidnapped, and he was a suspect, he thought bitterly. Why not? He'd been guilty of the sin of falling in love with the Borgadeux heiress, and for that, he supposed, he deserved to pay some sort of penance. As if he hadn't already.

The storm grew more violent as they reached Clearwater, and he wondered how the Australian could see through the drenched glass. The windshield wipers worked furiously but the rain pounded too hard. The idea that he had gotten into Borgadeux's car with two of his thugs, and was sitting quietly while they drove him into the worst part of the storm, for some unknown reason and some unknown destination, enraged him.

"If you don't let me contact my lawyer the minute we get where we're going," he shouted over the noise of the storm, "I swear to God I'll slap you with the biggest lawsuit you've ever seen."

"Just sit tight," the detective called over his shoulder. "You're in no trouble. You won't need a lawyer."

"Then what the hell is all this about?" Jeff asked. "You know, I could charge *you* with kidnapping! That is, if we don't get washed away by the storm."

He saw the sweat beading on Ben's brow as he tried to negotiate the Friday-evening traffic that the storm had done nothing but convolute even further. "Look, mate, I'd appreciate it if ya could shut up until I get us to Dunedin. This ain't no picnic, and if anything 'appens to this car, Borgadeux'll 'ave my ass."

"What's in Dunedin?" Jeff pressed, refusing to let up. "The Borgadeux live in Tampa."

They came to a traffic jam on Highway 19, one of the main arteries through Pinellas County, and Ben began massaging his temples. "There's somebody who wants t'talk t'ya," he said. "That is, presuming we ever get through this bloody 'ell t'get there."

"Well, if it's anybody in the Borgadeux family, male or female, I'll pass."

"No, ya won't. I ain't goin' through this for nothin'."

Jeff sat back and tried to rack his brain for some clarity. It was Leah who had sent for him, he told himself, even though it seemed more her father's way to have him dragged in like this. But what on earth would either of them want with him now?

Something to do with this kidnapping, he told himself, and he had to admit to some degree of curiosity.

They turned west on Curlew Road as the storm continued to rage around them. It was a bad one, he thought, unlike the isolated electrical storms they usually had in Florida. They reached the bridge cutting across the Gulf to Dunedin Beach and Honeymoon Island, and he sat up straighter.

A crack of lightning split the sky directly over them, its thunder coming simultaneously, as Ben slowed the Jaguar and pulled into the driveway of a small beach house behind a cluster of condominiums.

Ben opened the garage with a remote control, slipped the car in beside a minivan, and looked back over the seat as the door closed behind them. "Look, just cooperate for a few minutes, okay? You'll understand it all soon enough."

Wary of the whole situation, Jeff got out of the car and looked around him. "Whose house is this?"

"You'll see," Ben said, and started up the stairs to the door.

Lance Borgadeux opened the door, and his eyes shot with hateful arrogance to Jeff, as if he'd have liked nothing better than to beat the hell out of him for having had the gall—someone as low as him—to love his daughter. The feeling was mutual.

"Well, if it isn't old Borgy himself," Jeff said, feeling a new power now that he no longer cared what the man thought of him. He had nothing left to lose. "Long time no see."

Borgadeux didn't answer. Instead, as if for once he wasn't in control of things, he crossed his arms and looked toward the living room as Jeff came into the kitchen.

"His alibi checked out," the detective was saying. "But we brought 'im anyway, like she said."

Jeff looked past Ben into the living room, waiting for whatever—whyever—they had brought him here to be revealed. Leah stood there, her face paler than he'd ever seen it, her eyes swollen as if she'd just spent a lot of time crying and her blond hair disheveled and sticking to her damp face. But damn it all, she was still just as beautiful as the day she'd left him. He steeled himself for whatever was to come, and honestly wondered if he was ready for it. Under his breath, he muttered a curse and turned back to the kitchen.

"Jeff." Her voice was raspy with emotion.

Slowly, he turned back around, disgust distorting his face.

"What do you want?" he asked through stiff lips.

"I...I have to talk to you," she said. She looked past him, to the other men standing around him.

"Would you all please leave us alone for a few minutes? We have to talk alone."

"What happened, Leah?" he asked, not waiting for them to clear the room. "Did you convince your father that I wasn't worthless? Did you tell him to track me down and drag me back for another shot?" The cruel comment seemed to drain her more than he'd expected, and he almost regretted saying it. Almost.

Her father pushed through the others, his face a study in controlled rage. "Leah, please. You don't have to do this."

"Alone, Daddy," Leah said again, though the determined word came on a flat monotone. "I'll call you when we're finished."

The door to the kitchen closed behind Jeff, and their eyes met and held for a painful stretch of eternity. She was still fragile, he thought. Still so breakable. And damn it, so was he.

He waited, but she made no move to speak, and finally his eyes fell to the blanket she had wadded under her arm, and the worn-out bunny she held against her chest. He met her eyes again, desperate and despairing, and forced himself to ask.

"What am I doing here, Leah?" The question came out impatiently, but some niggling panic began to rise up inside him as the second question came to his lips. "Who is Cassandra Borgadeux, and why the hell did they think I kidnapped her?"

Leah held herself still for a moment, and he thought she would never answer. Finally, she drew in a deep, quick sob. "She's my daughter," she whispered, almost too low to hear. "And you, Jeff . . . You're her father."

Chapter Two

For a moment, the words refused to sink in, and Jeff stood staring at her, his face blank and pale. Finally, slowly, the realization washed over him.

"What the hell are you talking about?" The question came out on a raspy whisper, and he took a step closer to her.

Tears crept into Leah's eyes. "I call her Casey. She's two years old, Jeff, and she looks like you, and she's the—"

Jeff held out a hand to stem the stream of information that seemed so incongruous, so unexpected, and reached out to a chair to steady himself. His face reddened, and his words shredded through tight lips. "Are you telling me...that you had a baby? *My* baby?"

Crumpling beneath the question, Leah brought the blanket to her face. "I'm so sorry, Jeff. I tried to tell you. You wouldn't take any of my calls."

"That was because you dumped me!" he shouted. "You didn't tell me you were pregnant!"

"I didn't know then," she shouted back. "Jeff, I found out after I left you. But by then you hated me...."

Her words seemed to blur into some unintelligible whirlwind of memories and pains that circled through Jeff's mind like a tornado ready to sweep him out of existence. He shook his head, remembering her expressionless face when she'd ended things with him, the countless calls he'd refused to take, the endless, sleepless nights. He looked up at her and saw that her tears were flowing harder. "So that let you off the hook? A few foiled attempts to contact me? For God's sake, Leah, you could have left a message! I would have answered if I'd known you were pregnant! Was that too easy for you?"

"I couldn't do it that way!" she screamed. "I tried to tell you in person, myself, but finally I convinced myself that it was better if you didn't know!"

"Better for who, Leah? The baby? Am I some horrible monster that has to be kept from my child?"

"No!"

"Was it better for you, then? Better for your almighty father? Would it have cramped your style to admit to your child that her father was a man with calluses on his hands?"

"No! I was confused and hurt and panicked! I didn't want to hurt anymore!"

"And it's always easier to fall back into your father's cushy prison, isn't it, Leah, and the big bad world just goes away?"

"No, Jeff! You've got it all wrong. It wasn't that way."

"Wasn't it?"

"No! I haven't lived with my father since I was pregnant. I live here, alone with Casey. I support myself and it's not always easy and cushy. And if you look around, you'll see that the only thing that's gone away is my *daughter! That's* the benefit of being a Borgadeux, Jeff. And I never asked for it!"

The rage and emotion and terror behind her words stunned him, and at once the reason for his being brought here hit him full force.

"Kidnapped." The word rolled from his lips on a note of horror, and he stepped toward her and grabbed her arms. "Your baby...*my* baby. She's been kidnapped?"

"Yes!" Leah's own terror distorted her face, and he felt her trembling beneath his touch as she clung tighter to the blanket and worn bunny. "She was snatched from the baby-sitter's this afternoon, and the kidnappers left this ransom note. That's why my father's here. I don't have that kind of money—"

Jeff let go of her, his rough release making her stumble back. He snatched up the note and read the fateful words that had been glued onto the page like something in a B movie. The words were filled with venom that could mean the end of his daughter. The daughter he'd never even seen.

His heart rate sped to an all-time high, and he sank onto a couch, dropped his face into his hands. A daughter. His daughter. Kidnapped.

A misty glaze filled his eyes when he ran his fingers down his face and looked up at Leah again. "How long has she been gone now?"

"About six hours," she whispered. "And she doesn't have her blanket . . . and she has asthma. She needs medication, Jeff. She must think I abandoned her. . . . She must be terrified . . . and this damn storm . . ."

He swallowed and tried to calm his whirling thoughts, quiet his tumultuous emotions. "What . . . what are they doing? Is anybody looking for her? Have they questioned anyone?"

"Of course," she whispered. "That's how you got into this, remember?"

He didn't answer, but reached out and took the bunny from her hands. He looked down at it, saw the worn fur and the dirty whiskers, and a newer, more profound sense of loss than he'd ever felt washed over him. "Why did you decide to tell me now?" he whispered without looking at her. "You could have just had me questioned without letting them tell me."

"You would have gotten curious. You would have found out." She swallowed, and a sobbing moan sounded in her throat. "Besides, I needed for you to know. I'm so scared. . . ." Her words broke off on a sob, and he brought his eyes back up to hers. But he didn't comfort her.

"Look, I don't expect anything of you," she said when she could speak again. "Casey and I are doing fine on our own. Nothing really has to change because you know."

His expression grew harder, more strained, but still he only stared at her, clutching the bunny in his hands.

The door to the living room opened, and Lance Borgadeux stepped inside, not hiding the fact that he'd listened to every word of their conversation. "Now you know, Hampton. You're free to go now. My people will drive you back."

"The hell they will." Jeff met Borgadeux's eyes across the room, his as steady and unwavering as the tycoon's. "I'm staying here."

"Oh, no, you're not." Borgadeux started toward him, but Jeff came to his feet, undauntingly facing him. "You're not needed here anymore. We're in the middle of a crisis, and the last thing we need is you hanging around—"

"Daddy, stop it," Leah cut in.

"I'm staying if I have to break somebody's neck to do it!" Jeff bit out, his eyes reflecting his willingness to do just that.

"Is that a threat?" Borgadeux asked, amused. "Are you threatening me?"

"Take it anyway you want, pal. You had me dragged here against my will, remember? And now you spring this little revelation on me as an after-thought, and I'm supposed to run along back home like nothing ever happened?"

"If you want me to use force, Hampton, I have three capable detectives in there who can do it."

"Stop it!" Leah came between her father and the father of her child. "If Jeff wants to stay, he can stay. He has every right."

"To do what?" her father demanded. "Hang around here and get in the way?"

"I'm staying," Jeff said through his teeth again, his voice quivering with rage. "I've just been told that I have a daughter, and that she's been kidnapped. At the moment, I'd think you'd have more important things on your mind than me. If not, then maybe I should make a few calls and get my own detectives working on the case."

"That won't be necessary." Borgadeux took a step backward, breathed a heavy, long-suffering sigh and gave in. "All right, Hampton, you stay. But if you start to get in the way or upset my daughter any more than she already is, so help me God, I'll throw you out of here myself."

"And when you start getting in the way and upsetting your daughter, do I get to throw *you* out, Borgy?"

Again, Leah stepped between them. "Dad, just let it go, all right? We have to concentrate on Casey. She's the most important thing right now."

"Yeah." Her father started toward the door, where the detectives were waiting for him to call them to his aid, but he didn't remove his threatening eyes from Jeff. "I suppose what Leah needs right now is a nice little distraction, anyway. You're good for that, if nothing else."

The hateful comment hit its mark, silencing Jeff, and he turned his cold eyes back to Leah as her father left the room.

For a moment, they stared at each other, her eyes still wet with tears, her hands still shaking as she clutched the blanket.

"Just for the record," Jeff said in a steady, controlled monotone, "I'm not staying here to butt egos with your father, or to comfort you, or to distract you. I'm staying here because I have a little girl who I've never even met, who's in the hands of God-knows-what right now. And despite how you'd like for me to go along as if nothing has happened, I can't walk out of this now."

"I know that," she whispered. She went to the piano in the corner, to the framed picture of the little girl, and brought it back to him. Tears filled her eyes again. "I'd give anything if I could hand her to you, and introduce you and let you see how beautiful and wonderful she is. But all I have for now is a picture."

His lips trembled, and he wet them and took the picture. His brows came together as he stared at it, and she saw the fine mist forming in his eyes. Slowly, he dropped back to the couch and pinched the bridge of his nose. "I'll never forgive you for this, Leah," he whispered.

"I don't expect you to."

Not taking much comfort in her response, he let his eyes fall back to the picture in his hand, to the image of the little package of life with sunshine and rainbows in her eyes. He had already missed two years—the most crucial ones, according to psychologists—and now she was a little lady with a personality, a vocabulary, likes and dislikes. But he didn't know what any of them were.

Bonding…it was a word that had meant little to him a few hours ago. Now it meant the world…for he had missed doing so with his daughter.

But as he set down the picture and looked at the bunny again, the reality of what had brought him here hit home once more. Some stranger had taken his child.

Suddenly an urgency like he had never known washed over him. He looked up at Leah, and saw the terror swimming just beneath the surface of her eyes. And he shared it.

The phone rang, startling them both, and Leah punched the On button to the cordless phone and quickly brought it to her ear. In the kitchen, the recording equipment switched on and the three detectives began trying to trace the call by way of their cellular phones.

"Hello?" Her voice quivered.

"Leah? Have you found her yet? What's going on?"

Letting out a disappointed breath, Leah put her hand over the receiver. "It's just Anna, Casey's babysitter."

She watched Jeff wilt, then get up from the sofa and walk into the kitchen, where every word of the conversation was being taped, anyway. From the speaker on the recorder, he could hear the conversation.

"Leah? Are you there?"

Leah went back to the phone. "Yes, Anna, I'm here. And no, we haven't found her. We thought you might be the kidnapper."

She heard a sob on the other end of the connection, and instantly imagined Anna with wet, swollen eyes and her fingers forever plowing through her red curls. "I can't believe this," she cried. "I can't believe this could happen. Anna, I hadn't given her her afternoon dose of theophylline when they took her. What if—"

Leah's face contorted, and again, she brought the blanket to her face.

"Please," Anna said, "can't I come over and wait this out with you? You shouldn't be alone...."

"I'm not alone." Her eyes collided with Jeff's as he stood in the kitchen doorway; and she saw the coldness in them and shivered. "Besides, I want someone to be home at your house. Since that's where they got her...."

Her voice trailed off as the possibility that it had all been a mistake, that they had taken the wrong child, that they might not even know where to contact her, flitted through her mind.

"All right," Anna said with a shaky sigh. "Please, just keep me informed, huh? I can't stand this. I feel so responsible."

Leah closed her eyes and tried to stifle the memory of her reaction that afternoon when she'd first confronted Anna after being told about the kidnapping.

How could you be so irresponsible? How could you let a strange man put my baby in his car? It's all your fault!

Instead of defending herself, her baby-sitter and closest friend had pulled her into her arms, weeping as deeply and desperately as she had.

It had only taken a few minutes for Leah to come to her senses and apologize, for she knew that Anna would have laid down her life to protect the child.

"You're not responsible," Leah said now, meaning it. "It was going to happen anyway. They just used you."

"Leah, if there's anything you can think of for me to do, please..." Her voice cracked, but she went on. "I told that detective everything I know. But I panicked and didn't see the license plate.... Damn it, why didn't I see the license plate?"

Leah saw Jeff turn back toward her as he listened to the conversation playing in the kitchen, and the softness, the worry, the vulnerability in the eyes that could be at once hard and soft, cold and warm, touched her heart. Behind that hard, angry shell, she knew the old Jeff still resided. "Anna, I'll let you know as soon as I hear something." Her voice lacked its usual energy, and a soul-deep weariness kept the tone flat and lifeless.

"Yeah, I guess you have to keep the line open, huh?"

Leah didn't tell her that she had Call Waiting, and that any call would come through anyway. "Yeah, but I'll call you later."

She hung up the phone, stared down at it and looked up again to see Jeff at the doorway looking at her. He had been working that day, she realized in one of those random thoughts that the mind struggles toward in moments of crisis. His jeans—tight and faded over every curve and bend of his body—were dusty at the knees, and his blue work shirt, its sleeves rolled up at the elbow, bore various unidentifiable smudges. His hands—hands she remembered as strong and big and protective, so rough across her skin, though his touch was always nothing short of tender—looked dry and rough as he folded them under his arms. As if he sensed her thoughts, he drew his eyes away from her and back to the detectives in the room behind him.

"Why did you tape that call?" he asked. "Do you suspect the baby-sitter?"

"At this point, everyone's suspect, mate."

"She didn't have anything to do with it," Leah said, coming into the kitchen. "She's the best friend I have, and she's as upset as I am about what happened. She blames herself."

"She *should* blame herself," her father interjected. "The kid was abducted while she was taking care of her. I wouldn't be surprised if she set the whole thing up. Figured she'd take the opportunity to squeeze a little out of the Borgadeux while she had the chance."

"She didn't do that, Dad," Leah snapped. "I wouldn't have left Casey with someone like that. She's a good, caring person, and I trust her."

"Yeah, well, we know what kind of pathetic judge of character you are, don't we?" her father flung back.

"I've done just fine for two years!"

"And look how it wound up! You don't know where your daughter is and I'm the only one who can bail you out of this. Independence isn't all it's cracked up to be anymore, is it?"

Jeff looked from Leah to her father, trying to stay detached from either of the people who sent his emotions rocketing in different directions. He saw the toll her father's words had taken on her, when she already looked ready to collapse. For some unfathomable reason, that made him angry.

"Independence has nothing to do with this, Dad," she said through her teeth. "And if you don't mind, I've had enough of your accusations and observations."

She left the room, ending the argument, and Jeff watched, stunned at what he'd seen. In the past, she had cowered from her father, but now...

Silence engulfed the kitchen in her wake, and finally, Jeff gave Borgadeux a look of disgust and went into the living room.

The storm had calmed and the rain had slowed to a drizzle, but still the surf pounded against the shore in a frothy display of fierceness.

Jeff looked toward the hallway where Leah had gone. Some indeterminate force drew him that way, and he wrote it off to simply feeling alone and needing more information. Slowly, he walked into the hallway and checked the master bedroom on the left. The room was feminine and pink, and it smelled of her unique scent—a scent that he doubted she had bought in a store. It was a sent that floated around her like an aura, lingering in rooms she passed through, trapping itself in his clothes... and his memory.

She wasn't there, so he stepped to the door directly across from it, and saw her sitting on a frilly little Mickey Mouse bedspread draped over a twin bed that had a wooden rail on the side. Her feet were crossed Indian-style on the bed, and suddenly she looked very young and lost. He stepped into the room and leaned back against the Humpty Dumpty wallpaper, watching her.

"Why are you letting him stay here with you when he talks to you like that?" he asked.

She pulled her feet up and hugged her knees. Still, she clutched the blanket as if it, alone, could keep her bond to her daughter intact. He went to a white rocker in the corner, sat down and settled his elbows on his knees. A strange, warm feeling came over him, and he tried to picture the little girl he'd seen in the living room photographs lying asleep on that bed, sitting on the floor amid the Lego blocks in the corner, rocking in her mother's lap in that chair....

"She's so shy...and she gets spooked easily." Leah's voice cracked on a high-pitched note and her face twisted as she pushed out the words. "New situations...new people...always frighten her. She only feels safe with me and Anna. What must she be feeling right now? What must she be thinking?"

Jeff met her eyes.

She held up the blanket, shook it. "This blanket...she drags it around everywhere...holds it against her face and sucks her thumb. They could have at least taken it with her...so she'd have something familiar. Something that didn't scare her to death...."

She dropped her face into the wadded blanket, and the sobs that shook her shoulders frightened him. He got up, the chair creaking with the release of his weight, and he stepped toward her. "Listen, why don't you lie down? Try to get some rest. It could be a long night."

"Can't...I can't sleep when my baby's out there...."

"Then don't sleep," he said. "Just stay here where it's quiet for a while. Lie down and just rest." Gently, he set his hand on her shoulder and urged her down to the pillow.

When her head sank into the Mickey Mouse pillow sham, she looked up at him, her eyes raw and wet, her nose shiny and red, and for a moment he forgot his own pain, his bitterness toward this woman. He wanted to slide his arms around her, hold her against him and make all her problems his. Would it be that easy to forgive when he'd so carefully cultivated his hatred of her? Was he really that weak? Or were his emotions simply that strong—that disloyal to his own cutting memories?

He saw a soft comforter folded on a toy chest in the corner of the room, and taking it, shook it out and laid it over her.

"Thank you, Jeff," she whispered.

His throat constricted, and he found he couldn't answer. Instead, he nodded, and quietly backed out of the room. At the door, he stole one last look at her, wondering how a woman could look both tormented and beautiful at the same time, and how a man could feel both weak and strong. She had always made him feel that way—as though he were strong enough to protect her from any harm that came her way, yet powerless where his heart was concerned.

He saw a tear roll over her nose and drop on the hand cradled under her face. And feeling his power slipping away too quickly, he left her alone in his daughter's room.

BACK IN THE KITCHEN, Ben was talking on a cellular phone to one of his agents in the field. Listening, Jeff stepped back into the room where Lance Borgadeux leaned against the counter, reading the stock section of the newspaper. Willy, the other detective, studied a notepad on which he had jotted a conglomeration of scribbled notes.

"What's going on? Have they found anything?"

"Not yet. The baby-sitter seems clean."

Jeff pulled out a chair and sat down. Propping his elbows on his knees, he rubbed his face. "This is all so overwhelming." He looked at the men over his fingertips, and sat up straight. "I couldn't get enough from her. She's too upset. What exactly happened when the baby was kidnapped?"

Willy flipped back through his notepad. "Apparently, the child was playing in a sandbox in the front yard, when two men drove up in a car. One of them got out and asked the sitter for directions. As she was giving them, the man leaned over and picked up the child."

"Didn't the baby-sitter think that was strange?"

"According to our witness—a neighbor who was also out in her yard—she told him to put her down. At that point, the man took off for the car with the girl. Sounds like it was all planned. They knew who they wanted, where she'd be, how to best grab her—"

"God." Jeff got up again, raking his hand through his hair. "This is unbelievable." Ben hung up his phone, and Jeff turned to him. "The note. How did they leave the note?"

"It was stuffed into a pop bottle, and they threw it out the window as they took off."

Jeff stared down at the surveillance equipment set up on the table, sorting through the ugly facts and trying to make some sense of it. He thought of Jan, back at the work site, and his crew still scratching their heads and wondering why two detectives rode off with their boss. He pointed to one of the cellular phones. "Mind if I make a call? I need to tell my sister that I'm not being tortured."

Ben handed him the phone. "Sure, mate."

Dreading the call, Jeff dialed the number. The line was busy, and he surmised that his sister/secretary was on the phone telling everyone in town what had happened. Moaning, he clicked the button and dialed the other office number. It rang.

"Hello?"

"It's me, Jan."

"Jeff! Are you all right? Hold on."

He smiled when she put him on hold, presumably to hang up on her gossip-buddy, and thanked his stars that the call wasn't an emergency. In seconds, she was back.

"Jeff? Where are you?"

"I'm in Dunedin at Leah Borgadeux's house."

"Leah's?" He could hear the censure in her voice. "What does *she* want?"

"She had a little bomb to drop on me," he said. "I'll tell you all about it later. Just wanted to let you know that I'm going to be here for a while. Don't worry."

"Are they going to bring you back? Do you need me to pick you up?"

"No. I'll probably be here all night."

"Jeff, are you crazy? Do you have to be reminded how badly she hurt you?"

"No, Jan, I don't. It's not what you think." He sighed and rubbed his face. "Look, just close things down for me. I'll explain it all later."

He hung up the phone before his sister could protest further, and looked up to see that Borgadeux had folded his newspaper and had settled his steely eyes on Jeff.

"Where's Leah?" he asked.

"In Casey's room," Jeff said quietly. "She's lying down."

"Well, get her out of there. That's the last room she needs to be in right now."

"You care to explain why?"

"It's obvious to any moron," he said. "She needs to stay strong, not wallow in that room looking at all the things that remind her of Cassandra. It'll just feed her worry."

"I doubt seriously that she needs to be *reminded* of her daughter," Jeff threw back. "And I think it helps her to be around Casey's things."

"Who the hell cares what you think?" Borgadeux shouted. "Nobody asked you. As far as I'm concerned, you're an intruder right now in a very private family matter. So you can just sit there and keep your mouth shut—"

"Dad!"

The two men swung around and saw Leah standing in the doorway, a look of disgust and impatience coloring her pale features. "I'm getting real tired of hearing the two of you bicker. My nerves are already shot, and you two aren't helping—"

The phone shrilled, startling everyone in the room, and catching her breath, Leah grabbed it up.

"Hello?" Her voice came out raspy and unstable.

Jeff looked at Ben, who wore a pair of headphones through which he now monitored the phone call since Leah was in the same room, and from the look of him, Jeff could tell that it was the call they'd been waiting for. The call from the bastard who had kidnapped his child.

Chapter Three

"Do you have the money?"

Leah steadied herself and tried to control the overwhelming nausea taking hold of her. "Yes. Yes, I have the money. Where is my daughter? What have you done with her?"

Jeff stepped closer to Leah, putting his face next to the phone to hear the man who was speaking. He felt her arm trembling, and she swayed slightly, as though she might faint. With one hand, he touched her back to steady her.

"Shut up and listen if you ever want to see her again. I want you to deliver the two million to me at midnight tonight. And you'd better come alone, or you'll never see the kid alive again."

Before Leah could answer, Jeff snatched the phone from her hand. "Listen to me, you bastard," he said. "I'm Jeff Hampton, Casey's father, and if Leah's going anywhere tonight, I'm going with her. If you think she's going to walk into a trap—"

The phone cut off, and Jeff stood holding the receiver in his hand, listening to the dial tone hum in his ear.

"No!" Leah's scream shook the house. Her face turned a raging red, and she swung her fist against his arm. "How could you do that? Do you know what you've done? You've made them mad and let them know that I've brought someone into this! They could kill her for this!"

Jeff slammed down the receiver. "I was trying to help. I couldn't go with you without their permission, Leah, because they might see me. But if I told them—"

"Told them?" she repeated. "Jeff, we're not going anywhere now. I've waited *hours* for that phone call, and they never even got the chance to tell me where to deliver the money!" Her voice broke off on a sob, and shaking her head, she collapsed into a chair. "I can't believe you did that!"

Jeff turned around and confronted the men at the table. Ben was on the cellular phone, scrambling to get the call traced. The other two rewound the tape and listened through the headphones.

Only Borgadeux took the time to bore a lethal look through Jeff. "Why don't you get the hell out of here, Hampton, before you wind up getting the kid killed?"

"Why don't you get off my back!"

"Shut up, both of you!" The piercing order came from Leah, who then got to her feet and ran through the living room, out the glass doors and onto the balcony overlooking the Gulf.

Jeff stood paralyzed with remorse and defeat as he faced the man he despised so. Borgadeux only stared at him.

At last, Willy broke the silence. "We traced the call to a phone booth, and I put in a call to one of our men near that area. They just got there, and it's empty. We missed him."

"Damn." Ben stood up and paced across the room, trying to think. "Okay, don't anybody panic. The guy won't give up that easy. For two million, 'e'll call back. You can count on it."

"I didn't think the guy would hang up," Jeff said through his teeth. "I just couldn't believe you guys were going to even consider letting her deliver that money alone. And I figured if I was up-front about who I was..."

"We *weren't* goin' to let 'er go alone," Ben snapped. "We would 'ave tailed 'er the whole time to make sure she wasn't in danger."

"But that would be even more dangerous than what I just did," Jeff argued. "If they spotted you, it could jeopardize everything. Don't you see that if they knew I was coming, I could help protect her and my being there wouldn't jeopardize anything?"

"Your being here has *already* jeopardized everything," Borgadeux shouted.

Jeff turned back to the detectives, but they were already on the telephone, listening to the headphones, or typing things into a lap-top computer. He went to the door, looked out across the living room to the glass doors of the terrace and saw Leah, standing distraught on the wet deck.

He couldn't remember the last time he'd felt so low. Yes, he could, he amended. It was the last time he'd seen Leah Borgadeux, when he'd let her walk out of his life.

But this time it was by his own hand. He had screwed up big-time. He had acted on a gut instinct, but it had served him wrong.

Slowly, he started across the living room to the terrace. Sliding back the glass door, he stepped out to join Leah.

The air was thick with the smell of saltwater and rain, and the pounding of the shore provided little peace. Leah leaned against the wet rail, staring out over the angry Gulf. She made no move to look at him.

"Leah, I'm sorry I did that. I didn't mean—"

"If you knew her...if you cared about her...you wouldn't have risked that. You'd realize how much was at stake."

"I don't know her because you haven't let me."

"That's not the point." She flung around, facing him with raging tears and a mottled face. "The point is that this is not a game. This is my baby's life. You can't take things upon yourself like you just did." Her voice broke, and she brought the child's blanket up to muffle a sob. "Damn it, Jeff, if anything happens to her, I don't know what I'll do. She's all I have. She's everything...."

The phone rang again, like a torturous device that strangled the life from Leah's soul. Shooting past him, she ran to the extension in the kitchen. Sniffing to clear her voice, she whispered, "Hello."

Jeff followed her in, but this time he stood back, feeling like the intruder Borgadeux had accused him of being.

"Yes...yes, I understand but...please, can I speak to her? Just so I'll know she's all right? Please!"

The phone went dead, and holding it in her hand, she lowered it from her ear. "He hung up. I didn't get to tell them about the asthma!"

The detectives scrambled to trace the call, but this time the kidnapper hadn't been on the line long enough.

"What did he say?" It was Borgadeux who asked.

"He said that he would call me back at midnight to tell me where to deliver the money, and that if I do as they say, I'll get Casey back then." She threw Jeff a dull, heartless look. "And he said that Jeff could come with me, as long as he's unarmed. But if anyone else follows me or comes with me, they'll kill Casey."

Relief burst out of Jeff's lungs.

"Good goin', mate," Ben acknowledged, patting Jeff's back. "Guess you were right. We'll put a phone in the van, and you can call us the moment you 'ave Casey. We'll be close enough by to get there in time to apprehend them." Jeff didn't hear, for his gaze was locked with Leah's, assessing her for some sign that she didn't still blame him for interrupting the first call. "I'm glad Leah won't 'ave to go alone," Ben went on. "I didn't want to say anything, but I was a little worried they might think two Borgadeux would command higher ransom than one."

Borgadeux massaged his temples. "Oh my God. You don't think—"

"It won't happen." Jeff's words were issued with a note of finality that Leah couldn't deny. "I won't let anything happen to her."

Reluctantly, Leah looked him in the eye, noting the protective way he was prepared to come to her rescue. Something warm, secure, hatched inside her, but the fear still gnawed at her heart. "No more heroics? No more risks?"

"None. I swear it."

Relieved that he'd done what he'd done, but unable to reveal that relief so soon after her accusations, she nodded and wiped her face. "Okay. Then all we can do now is wait."

"You need to eat something," Borgadeux said. "It's going to be a long night. We all need to."

"I can't eat, Dad."

"You have to make yourself."

That taut, cliff-edge expression returned to her face. "If you're hungry, Dad, you know where the refrigerator is." Then drawing in a deep sigh, she left the room.

Jeff watched her go, and feeling the sudden chill of abandonment, left the kitchen and walked to the sliding glass doors, where the rain was beginning to fall harder.

It had worked, he told himself. His instincts had served him right, and he would be there to protect Leah when she delivered the money.

So why did he still feel like he'd blown it?

The thought of how dangerous these kidnappers could be forced perspiration to break across his forehead, and reaching up to massage his temples, he turned around and looked toward her bedroom. He saw her come out and disappear into the bathroom. He heard the door lock, and the sound of the shower being turned on.

Without realizing what he was doing, he walked slowly toward the bathroom, stopped just outside it, and tried to imagine her inside, unzipping those tight pants she wore, sliding them down over her hips, stepping out of them with those long, silky legs. He could envision her blouse slipping over her flat stomach, the soft indention of her navel, the small breasts just big enough to fill his hands....

He wondered if she'd had a man since him, if any other had touched and loved her, if they had tasted the sweetness of her skin....

His throat went dry, and sliding his hands into his pockets and hauling in a deep breath, he went into Casey's room and recalled Leah lying there on Casey's bed, crying, sick with worry for her baby....

His baby...

Slowly, he stooped in the corner where the Lego blocks were scattered on the floor, and picked up one. He wondered if Leah played with her, if she taught her how to build towers and robots, if she praised her scribbled drawings, if she adorned her hair with big bows and dressed her in frilly dresses.

Sitting on the floor and leaning back against the wall, he let his eyes roam over the books in the red bookcase. Two photo albums caught his gaze, and quickly he reached for them. Opening the first one, he saw Casey's very first picture. She lay in Leah's arms, all red and blotched and beautiful, and Leah was smiling as tears rolled down her face.

Something painful twisted his heart, and he felt the sting of his own tears.

And as he turned the pages and saw all the moments with Casey he had missed, one of those tears fell to his stubbled cheek.

STEPPING INTO the warm spray of water, Leah closed her eyes and let the heat wash over her, calming her tense muscles and washing away the tears that had created a salty film over her skin.

She would see Casey tonight. In just a few hours, she would deliver the money where they said, and Casey would be back in her arms. If nothing went wrong.

But the truth was that all sorts of things could go wrong. Her father could intervene and ruin everything, or the detectives could follow without her knowledge and cause the whole thing to blow up. Or Jeff could lose his temper and either frighten the kidnappers away or make them angry. Or the kidnappers could just get cold feet, and decide to kill the whole plan.

And Casey, too.

Even as she washed the old tears away, new ones formed in her eyes and mingled with the water spraying on her face.

She wondered if Jeff realized how badly he had frightened her when he'd grabbed the phone. Already, nothing was in her control. Already, she was at the whim of the criminals who had Casey. When Jeff had done that, it was like he had deliberately and mercilessly severed the link between her and Casey.

He had only been trying to help, she told herself. Just like her father and the detectives were trying, and even though Jeff really *had* helped, it didn't settle her knotted stomach or calm the pounding in her head. It didn't make it any easier—right now—knowing that there were still hours to go before Casey would be safe.

There was no relaxing, she realized finally. Not while her baby was in a stranger's hands. Not until she had her safely back.

Stepping out of the shower, she dried her skin with a big towel, then slipped into her bedroom and dressed quietly in a big sweatshirt and jeans. Unable to join the others just yet, she went back to Casey's room.

Jeff was already there, huddled on the floor in a corner, looking at Casey's photo albums, studying pictures of the little girl who looked so much like him. His face held a poignant longing, a look that made Leah's heart melt into her toes, a look that revealed to her how good it was to share Casey with someone else who could love and appreciate her.

Slowly, she went to sit on the floor beside him. For a moment he didn't stir, and made no indication that he knew she was in the room with him. His eyes were glued to a recent picture of the child holding a Tootsie Pop, her face covered in sticky red candy. Instead of the smile she might have expected at such a comical portrait, she saw a fine mist glistening in his eyes.

"She loves Tootsie Pops," Leah said. "She always winds up getting it in her hair. Little pieces of it stick to her face, and her hands are covered with candy when she's finished. I usually have to bathe her right away."

He turned the page, and saw a picture of her at her first birthday party. Several other babies sat around the table in pointed hats, staring covetously at the birthday cake decorated with Minnie Mouse.

"Those are some of the kids from her Sunday-school class," she said. "And this one—" she pointed to a little boy of the same age as Casey "—he's Anna's son. They were born a week apart. That's how I met Anna. We were in the same Lamaze class. Her husband is in the Coast Guard and was gone a lot, so we helped each other. We got to be good friends."

He brought puzzled eyes to her, and Leah knew he was probably thinking how strange that was, since she had never had close friends before. She had been so sheltered...so protected...so smothered.

"When I went into labor, Anna went to the hospital with me and acted as my coach. She was the second person to ever hold Casey."

He frowned down at the pictures again. "I'm surprised your father didn't throw her out and insist on being there himself."

"I didn't call him until it was all over," she said. "I knew he'd just make me nervous and drive the hospital staff crazy. I kept it to myself until I was back home with Casey the next day. He wanted me to move back in with him, so I decided that the faster I got Casey settled at home, the easier it would be to convince him we were fine.''

"And did you? Convince him, I mean?"

"No," she said with a smile. "He still harasses me about it. Every single day he has some new reason why I would be better off to move back."

Jeff turned the page, and saw a picture of Casey in what looked like an oxygen mask. "What's this?"

A haunted look returned to her eye, and she stiffened again. "Her nebulizer mask. She's asthmatic, and sometimes I have to give her breathing treatments to help her breathe." Tears filled her eyes again, and she covered her mouth with her hand. "She was wheezing this morning. After I medicated her, she was fine, but I shouldn't have taken her to Anna's. I had an appointment with a woman putting together a trousseau, but I should have canceled it and closed the shop and kept her home...but she was breathing fine by the time I took her. When she gets upset—"

"I was asthmatic when I was a child," Jeff whispered, cutting her off. He brought his fingers to his eyes and pressed hard.

"That explains where she got it," she said. "You outgrew it?"

"Yeah, I outgrew it," he said in a tight voice. "I also had nosebleeds at night, I'm allergic to poison oak and my family has a history of diabetes. Those are things that a parent needs to know about her child's genes, don't you think?"

Leah felt the sting, and accepted it. "I would have told you if something serious like that had come up. I had always planned to tell you someday."

The idea seemed ludicrous, and he gaped at her with disbelief. "When? When she was grown and had children of her own? When you accidentally ran into me on the street? Or just when she was ill and you needed a kidney or something?"

"I told you today," she said. "You know now."

"Yeah. Now I know." He looked back down at the child's picture, and shook his head. "Only I can't figure out what I ever did to make you hate me so much."

Leah caught his arms and made him look at her. "I *never* hated you, Jeff. Never."

"You couldn't keep something like this from me if you didn't hate me, Leah."

"I called you a hundred times. I left messages on your machine, with your secretary, with your friends. I went to your office and waited, but you wouldn't see me. I finally realized that *you* hated *me!*"

"Yes, I hated you," he shouted, flinging the album across the floor and getting to his feet. "I hated you because you walked out on me! I wasn't good enough for you or your family!"

Leah stood up and faced him across the room. "You've got it all wrong, Jeff. My family wasn't good enough for you. My father would have destroyed you. You were right on the verge of closing the Suncoast Dome deal. He said he could pull the rug right out from under you. He had important people in his back pocket, Jeff, and I knew he had the power and determination to bankrupt you."

"So you convinced yourself that you had made some supreme sacrifice for me? How magnanimous of you, Leah. How generous." His sarcasm died off, and he swung around. "It's a crock, and you know it. If you'd loved me, nothing your father said or did could have influenced you. And nothing you ever say will convince me that you kept my daughter from me for my own good."

"I thought my breaking up with you was for your own good. But then when I found out I was pregnant, I wanted you so much...." Her voice broke off into a sob, and she stepped toward him. "But it was you who put up a wall between us then."

"No, Leah, it was you! You're the one who robbed me of two years I will never get back! You're the one who robbed Casey of a father who could love her and protect her from those jackasses that have her right now. And it was all for a buck, wasn't it? So your father wouldn't cut you out of his will, or cut off your charge accounts. Was it worth it, Leah?"

Leah slapped away a tear rolling down her face, and without honoring him with an answer, turned away to pick up the photo album lying on the floor where Jeff had thrown it.

When her voice was calmer, more controlled, she gave him a searing look and pushed past him out the door. "You don't know what you're talking about," she whispered through quivering lips, and she left him standing alone in his daughter's room.

FOR THE NEXT SEVERAL hours, they avoided speaking to each other. The only thing to break the silence was the ring of the detectives' cellular phones in the kitchen, and her father's calls as he tried to conduct business as usual from her living room. Jeff found refuge on the wet deck, poring over the photo albums by the light of a single patio bulb around which a swarm of mosquitos bumped and buzzed, trying to fill the gaps of the past two years.

In the bedroom, Leah busied herself packing a duffel bag of things that Casey might need immediately when they found her. A change of clothes. Some diapers. Bunny Fu-Fu and her blanket. Her medication. The air compressor and nebulizer, in case they found her in respiratory distress. And two million dollars in cash.

It was nearing midnight when she took the bag and briefcase of money into the kitchen and gladly accepted the cup of coffee her father handed her.

"Sit down, sweetheart," Borgadeux told her. "I want to talk to you."

She picked up the cordless phone and held it near her face. "They're going to call soon, Dad. There's not much time."

"I know that," he said. "But I wanted to talk to you about what's going to happen after you get Casey back. I want you to come home with me. I have a room all decorated for her, and you can have your old room back. You'll have servants and nannies and guards, and you'll never have to worry about kidnappers or baby-sitters or struggling to make ends meet again."

Leah sat silent, expressionless, as her father rambled on, and when she glanced toward the door, she saw that Jeff had come in and was leaning against the kitchen door, listening.

"I don't struggle to make ends meet, Dad. Business is good, and I can provide for my daughter just fine. And I don't need servants."

Borgadeux's voice rose a decibel. "Are you going to deny that you need security? After all this? You would honestly go along as usual, knowing that little Casey is an open target? It's foolish, girl, to keep pretending like you're an ordinary person, when you're a Borgadeux. You can have the advantages of that. Don't be stubborn when your daughter's safety is involved."

Her temples began to throb harder, and she brought her fingers up to massage them. "Dad, I really can't think about all this right now. All I can concentrate on is this phone ringing and the kidnapper telling me where I can find my baby."

"I understand that," he said. "But I wanted to mention it to you, because you need to think about it. You need to have a battle plan when you bring Casey home... *if* you bring her home."

"If?" Her voice slipped on the word. "Dad, don't say that. I have to believe that everything's going to go fine tonight. Please—"

"We'll get her back," Jeff said, walking to her chair and setting his hand on her shoulder. "There's no if about it. I'm going to see my little girl tonight."

Thankful for his confidence and his secure touch, which she realized was more to rile her father than to comfort her, she watched her father shoot Jeff a dangerous look and rise from the table.

"As soon as I get her," she said, "I want a doctor to examine her to make sure they didn't hurt her. But I don't want to take her to the hospital. She'll need to be home." She looked up at her brooding father. "Dad, after we get Casey, would you call her pediatrician and see if he'll meet us back here?"

Borgadeux shrugged. "I'll call him right now."

"No. No one else can know until we get her back. *Then* you can call."

Before Borgy could respond, the phone rang, and Leah lunged for it.

"Hello?"

"Are you ready to turn the corner?" the voice asked.

"What corner?" she asked breathlessly.

"The corner in this nightmare. The one that determines whether you ever see your kid alive again."

Chapter Four

Leah swallowed back the sickness rising to her throat and tried to get the words out. "Yes, I'm ready. You can have the money...but please don't hurt her."

"Go to the phone booth at the corner of Belcher and Drew Street," the caller said. "Wait there for further instructions. And I'll tell you one more time, if you bring anybody other than the kid's father, she's dead. We know what he looks like. We've done our homework."

"All right." She clutched the phone tighter. "Please...is she all right? Is she wheezing or coughing? She's asthmatic, and she needs medication—"

"Belcher and Drew," he repeated, and hung up.

Leah's heart sprinted in her chest as she cut off the phone and turned to Jeff. "Are you ready?"

"Yes," he said, starting for the door.

Leah grabbed the duffel bag and briefcase that contained the money, and saw Borgadeux reach for his keys.

"Wait a minute," Leah said, swinging around. "What are you doing?"

"We're going to follow out of sight," Borgadeux said. "Ben put a tracer on your van so we would know where you're going to be. We'll be just a few blocks away. You can also take the cellular phone. Call us if you need us."

"No!" She stopped at the door, her heart pounding in terror. "Dad, this is dangerous. They might see you. If someone's watching the house and they see us all leave, they'll be suspicious."

"She's right," Ben said. "We'll have t'wait a few minutes before we go."

Borgadeux held back reluctantly. "I'm not going to sit around twiddling my thumbs."

"Yes, you are," Jeff said. "It's the only thing you can do."

"Dad, if you jeopardize this, so help me God, I'll never forgive you for it," Leah said. "If you're worried about getting your damn cash back, Casey's worth a hell of a lot more than two million dollars."

Borgadeux dropped into a chair as Leah and Jeff went to the garage and climbed into her van.

THE RIDE to the designated phone booth was quiet, for the prospect of what they were walking into, what Casey was already in the middle of, played havoc in their minds. It took twenty minutes to reach the booth, set conspicuously at what normally would have been a busy intersection. Now, at 12:30 a.m., the street was almost deserted.

Leah pulled into the gas station parking lot next to the booth and rolled down her window. She cut off her lights, leaving the van enveloped in the opaque darkness. The moon hid above a thick froth of clouds, blocking out all light, and it looked as if it could begin raining again at any moment.

"Should I get out?" she asked, breaking the silence.

"No. Just wait here until the phone rings. It could be a while. They would want to give us plenty of time to get here."

"Yeah." Her word came out on a whisper, and her eyes gravitated to the phone. "So what do we do in the meantime?"

"Wait, wait and wait some more."

"I'm getting good at that." She shoved her fingers through her hair, realized she was perspiring. Taking in a deep breath, she whispered, "This is worse than when I was nine and a half months pregnant without a sign of labor. I thought nothing could be worse than that."

"Casey was overdue?" he asked, drawing her attention from the phone.

"Yeah."

"I was late."

The soft words were almost inaudible, and Leah looked at him in the darkness. "What?"

"I was late. My mother carried me for almost ten months. Is that kind of thing genetic?"

"I don't know," she whispered.

He gazed out into the night, focusing on the haze around a street lamp a half block away, where moths and mosquitos swarmed. "Was it hard? Labor, I mean?"

She took in a deep breath. "Not too bad. It was over in about six hours and Anna was great. It was all worth it."

"What about afterward, when you came home? Wasn't anybody there to help you?"

"No," she said, her tone a little more defensive than she wanted. "But it was fine. I'm self-sufficient. I didn't need anybody."

"You didn't need anybody." He uttered the words on a dull, despairing note, and shook his head. "Leah, this may not be the time, but I have to know. Did it ever occur to you during all that to call me, that I could have been there for you? That I would have wanted to see my daughter born?"

That old familiar guilt surged through her. "Yes, it occurred to me, Jeff. A hundred times. And I always intended to. But I always lost my nerve."

"Lost your nerve? Are you kidding?"

A car drove by, its headlights illuminating the van, and Leah's gaze followed it out of sight. "Jeff, by then I had let so much time pass that I knew you'd be furious I hadn't told you earlier. I had planned to call you when I went into labor. I didn't have the courage, and afterward . . . well, it was all said and done, and it seemed too late to include you." Her gaze drifted to the phone again as sharp regrets scraped at her senses. "Jeff, I was selfish, I know, but you have to understand my state of mind."

"What was your state of mind, Leah? Tell me, because I'd really like to know."

She winced at his frigid tone. "I was out from under my father's thumb for the first time in my life. I was struggling to start a brand-new business. I was dealing with a pregnancy. I was angry at you—"

"Angry at me! For what?"

"I don't know."

"You don't know? Leah, if you were angry at me, you owe it to yourself if not to me to at least figure out why. What in God's name did you have to be angry at me about?"

She cursed herself for ever admitting to that strange, unreasonable emotion, but it was too late. Now she had to find a way to explain it.

"It's stupid," she said. "It's irrational."

"So what else is new? I'm listening."

"I was angry at you..." She faded out and looked at the phone again, willing it to ring, to interrupt the honesty that seemed so bent on coming, but it didn't. "... because you didn't fight for me. Because you let me walk out, and that was the end of it. I kept telling myself that if you really loved me, you'd have come after me."

"So that's what it was? Some kind of insane test? To see how much I cared?"

"No, that isn't what it was at all. I told you it was irrational. None of what I was feeling made sense. When I realized I was carrying your baby, I suddenly realized that nothing my father did was worth breaking up the family we had created together. And I wanted you back."

"But it blew up in your face, didn't it? I didn't want you anymore."

"No, you didn't. And I didn't want you just for the baby's sake if you didn't want me."

They both looked at each other across the van, both of them full of pain and heartache that would never easily be quelled. Another set of headlights passed, illuminating a sliver of tears in his eyes.

"I loved you," he said through stiff lips. "You knew that."

"And I loved you," she whispered. "As much as I knew how. But at the time, I didn't have a lot of experience with love. Just manipulation, and possession and emotional blackmail. It took Casey to teach me what real love is."

"But I didn't get that luxury," he whispered.

Silence filled the van again—surrounded it— wringing her heart and nerves tighter. She wished for the words that could heal the wounds, but she knew there were none. Above all, she wished the phone would ring, but it didn't. Finally, she brought her tense gaze back to Jeff. "Jeff, I swear, when this is all over, when I have my baby back with me again, I won't try to keep you out of her life. I want her to know her father. I've made terrible mistakes, and I can't change the past, but I can change now."

"Yeah, right," he said. "And what about when old Borgy threatens to huff and puff and blow my house down again? Are you going to throw me out again, for my own damn good? Or this time will I get a choice?"

"My father has no hold on me anymore," she said. "I told you . . . he wouldn't have been there today if I hadn't desperately needed his money. I didn't have anywhere else to turn."

"You could have turned to me."

"For two million dollars? You don't have that kind of—"

"I could have gotten it, Leah. But you wouldn't know that, would you, because you don't really know me anymore. I could have been there for my daughter. I could have come through for her."

"But I wouldn't have had the right to ask."

"No, you wouldn't have," he agreed. "But that wouldn't have mattered.

"After this," he went on, "your father's going to feel like you owe him. Like he has some kind of new hold on you."

"I can deal with that," she said. "But I can swear to you that nothing he ever does will keep you from seeing Casey... if you want to."

A moment of quiet followed, and they both watched the phone. It sat silent, mocking their anxiety. "Damn it, why won't they call?" she whispered.

She reached behind her seat and unzipped her duffel bag. "Oh, no. Did I remember to pack her blanket?"

"It's in there," he said quietly.

"What about the bunny? I was so distraught—"

"I checked," he said. "It's wrapped in the blanket. Just relax. It'll be over soon."

"When?" she shouted, surprising herself more than him. "When will it be over? Why don't they call?"

"I don't know," he whispered.

"Do you think we got the address wrong? Is it possible that we're at the wrong one?"

"No," Jeff said. "They're just making us sweat."

She brought her hands to her face, and felt her own fingers trembling. Her legs felt rubbery and shaky, and she feared that when the phone rang, she would collapse trying to get to it.

She opened the door and started to get out.

"What are you doing?"

"I'm going to stand beside the phone. I can't just sit here."

"No. It's not safe. I don't want you standing out there in the open."

"I have to do something! How long are we going to sit here?" She dropped her face in the circle of her arms over the steering wheel. "This is driving me crazy!"

It began to drizzle, the raindrops drumming against the roof of the van and beading on the windshield. "Raining again!" she cried. "And Casey's out in this wet night air, and they'll probably leave her alone somewhere in the rain and she'll be terrified and—"

Before she knew what was happening, Jeff's arms were around her, his big, comforting, calloused hands stroking her hair and her back as she wilted, sobbing, against him. "Shh. It's okay," he said. "It's all right."

For the first time in over two and a half years, in the secure embrace of Jeff Hampton's arms, Leah realized just how much she had lost. Instead of calming her misery, it only heightened it.

"We'll get her back," he whispered. "I promise. We're going to have her in just a short time, and we can take her home and rock her...."

The "we" uttered so naturally, so easily, calmed her spirit, for it had been a very long time since there had been anyone else to plan and hope and love with her. He could love Casey, she told herself. And Casey would love him.

Swallowing and breathing in a sob, she looked up at him. "Are you . . . are you sure? Will we get her . . . get her back?" The words hiccuped on the rise and fall of her sobs.

"I'm sure." He stroked the tears from her cheek, and she could feel his breath against her lips, see the reassurance in his eyes, feel the confidence in his heart. She saw him wet his lips, felt him narrowing the space between their faces. . . .

His lips grazed hers, so lightly that she almost couldn't feel it, but even so, the slight touch sent emotion shooting through her. He pulled back, looking at her with pain and a little surprise, as if he couldn't decide whether to push her away or kiss her fully.

Reaching up, she framed his face, feeling the stubble against his fingertips, and his lips came back to hers.

Something—some long-held passion that had simmered for years—boiled to the surface as their kiss deepened and their hearts pounded out of control. His touch sent tiny shock waves through her, making her nerves tingle and her senses reel. He shifted slightly, pulling her closer against him, and his fingers slid through her hair, down her back. . . .

And suddenly the phone rang, startling them as if they'd been caught breaking each other's heart again.

Catching her breath and forsaking his arms, Leah bolted out of the van and grabbed the telephone. Jeff was behind her in an instant, his face pressed close to hers, listening.

"Drop the briefcase with the money in the garbage bin beside the red bench at Osceola Park. It's behind the library."

"Will Casey be there? Will I see her then?"

"*If* you do as we say, and the money is all there, you can pick up the kid at the playground behind the First United Methodist Church on Drew Street. If we see any sign of your being followed, you'll find her dead."

"I'll do as you say," she blurted. "Please . . . don't hurt her."

The phone went dead, and she slammed it down and rushed back into the van.

"Let me drive," Jeff said.

"No," she argued. "I already know the way. I can get there faster."

Not arguing further, he jumped into the passenger seat and held on as they raced to the location where the money would be dropped.

The cellular phone in the van rang, and Jeff looked at her. "It's your father."

"Don't answer it," she said. "He'll want to know where we're going. I don't want him to know, or he might screw everything up."

She ran a red light, and Jeff touched her arm. "Take it easy or you'll attract the police. That's all we need."

"You're right." Her hands trembled as she clutched the steering wheel and forced herself to slow down. "Please, God, don't let them hurt her."

"It's going to be okay," Jeff said. "You have to believe that."

They reached the park, screeched to a halt, and leaving the van idling, ran together to drop the brief-case in the garbage can. Then, looking around for any sign of the kidnappers, they walked as quickly as they could back to the van, got in and started to drive away.

"Do you see anyone yet?" Leah asked Jeff as he strained to see out the back window. "No. Not yet."

"How will they get Casey there before we get there, if they haven't gotten the money yet? How could they do that?"

"You said two of them kidnapped her. They prob-ably have some kind of communication with each other." Losing sight of the park, he turned back around in his seat. "He's probably grabbing the case at this very moment and calling his accomplice to leave Casey."

"Alone? In the rain? She's afraid of the dark, Jeff! She'll be terrified. You know they won't hang around. They'll just leave her—"

"We'll be there," he said. "That's all that matters. In just a few minutes, we'll be there."

Despite her efforts to go slowly, Leah ran another two red lights. The cellular phone began to ring again, but this time there was no discussion. They both ig-nored it. After a moment, it stopped ringing.

"Oh, God. I just thought of something."

"What?"

"Didn't Dad say that they had put a tracer on the van? They would know where we've been, where we've stopped. They'd realize that we dropped the money off at the park. What if they go there, and the kidnapper sees them, before we can reach Casey?"

Jeff sat stiffer in his seat, and found that this time he could offer no reassurances. "Let's go ahead and call them. Tell them not to do it."

"Yeah, okay. We don't have to tell them where we're going. Just tell them how important it is for them not to go where we've been."

Leah grabbed the phone and began punching out the number her father had written and taped to the back of it. He answered on the first ring.

"Dad, we dropped the money."

"At Osceola Park? We're almost there."

"No! Dad, please don't go there! Please! They're leaving Casey in another location, and it all depends on their not thinking anyone's following us! Please, if I mean anything to you, if Casey does, don't go there!"

"All right. We're turning off."

Leah wilted in relief.

"Where are you going now?"

"I can't tell you. Not until this is over."

"Leah, we can help you! We can be nearby, just in case—"

"No, Dad. I don't want you to do anything until I have Casey back."

She hung the phone up, and flung it to Jeff. "We're almost there. That's the church, right up there."

Jeff strained to see the playground behind it. There were no cars. No lights. No sign of life.

Leah skidded into the parking lot, threw the van into Park, and jumped out, leaving the van running as she bolted toward the fence surrounding the playground. "Casey!"

Jeff was behind her in the rain, searching the shadows for any sign of the child, when suddenly they heard a hoarse, raspy wail from across the yard.

"Casey!" Opening the gate, Leah burst across the yard to the little sandbox where her daughter sat, crying her heart out, what was left of her voice squeaking with soul-deep hysteria.

Leah grabbed the child and crushed her against her, instinctively rocking her body to stop her anguished cry.

Chapter Five

Jeff stood, awestricken, as Casey clung to Leah with a desperate embrace. He watched as Leah rose, holding her, and her little ringlets bounced against her shoulders.

Stepping close, he reached out a shaky hand to touch her hair. It was soft, baby-silky, but it wasn't enough. He wanted to see her face, wanted to touch her hand, wanted her to cling to him as she clung to Leah. Desperately, he wanted to ask if she was okay, but his voice would not function.

Leah seemed equally paralyzed, standing with the crying child, but finally she rasped, "Let's get out of here."

Nodding and trying desperately not to let his own tears shatter, he took them both back to the van. Quickly, he got into the driver's seat and pulled the van out of the parking lot.

In the passenger seat, the child still trembled and clung to Leah, still crying as if the ordeal had not yet ended. "Shh. It's okay, pumpkin. It's all right now. Mommy won't let them take you again."

Her voice wobbled as she spoke, and Jeff came to a red light and looked over at the mother and child. Casey was so small, so fragile, it was hard to believe she was two. He wondered if she was hurt physically. He swallowed the emotional obstruction in his throat. "Is she okay?" he asked. "Any bruises? Cuts?"

Leah's face broke with her sob, and she shook her head. "Nothing I can see. She's all right, except she's wheezing a little. Thank God, she's all right." She pried Casey away from her just long enough to see her face. "Honey, did those people hurt you? Were they mean to you?"

"I want my mommy," the two year old cried. "They said no."

"Mommy's here now, sweetheart. Nobody's going to take you again. I promise."

"I want blankie."

Ignoring the light that had turned green, Jeff kept the van at a halt and grabbed the duffel bag. Quickly, he handed Leah the blanket, watched Casey grab it covetously, watched her wad it next to her face, between herself and Leah, and bring her little thumb to her mouth. It seemed only then that she noticed him, and letting out a fresh round of sobs, she buried her face in Leah's chest.

"I'm sorry," Jeff whispered as the van still idled at the green light. "Did I scare you?"

"I want my mommy!"

Leah held her tight and cast him an apologetic look.

"Tell her I won't hurt her," he said in a soft, unthreatening voice. "I won't even touch her." The absurdity of that promise struck him in the heart, and he leaned closer. "She needs her mommy. Don't you, Casey? And Mommy's not going anywhere."

Her cries quietened a little, but she still kept her face buried.

"Why don't we pull over for a minute until we can calm her down?" Leah said.

Unable to make himself take his eyes off of her, he pulled the van into the Winn Dixie parking lot beside them, and left it idling.

He picked up the Bunny Fu-Fu that had fallen out of the blanket and slipped from his seat. "You want your bunny?" he asked.

Slowly, Casey stole a look at him. He handed it to her, and she took it by the ear with her thumb-sucking hand.

"Are you okay now?" he whispered, his voice a raspy wave of emotion.

Casey nodded and, laying her head against Leah's chest, closed her eyes.

"She's tired," he whispered, and he looked up in the darkness and met Leah's eyes. Tears blurred his vision, but he blinked them back.

"I'd let you hold her," she said, "but she's a little too frightened right now."

"It's okay. There's plenty of time for that," he whispered.

The little girl opened her eyes again—eyes that he guessed were as red and raw and swollen as her mother's—and assessed the man who had given her her bunny.

"Casey," Leah said softly, brushing her damp curls back from her face. "I want you to meet Jeff. He's our good friend. And he's going to keep us safe."

Casey stared at him for a moment, then looked up at her mother. "Mommy not leave me?"

"No. I'll not leave you. I'm staying right here. We're going home."

Accepting the answer, Casey coughed and looked again at Jeff, stuffed her thumb back into her mouth and closed her eyes.

Tears rolled down Leah's face again, but she tried to hold back the sob for fear of further frightening the baby. "She'll never be the same," she whispered. "She'll never trust anyone again." The child coughed again, a wet, phlegmy cough, and Leah dropped her head down and listened to her breathing.

Jeff brought his hand to Casey's hair, but thought better of it. He had promised not to touch her. "She'll trust me," he whispered. "I'll make her trust me."

He moved his hand, and looked at the thumb beginning to fall out of the baby's mouth. "I think she's asleep."

Leah smiled and kissed the top of Casey's head. "I really need to give her a breathing treatment and her medication. Let's take her home, Jeff. It's all over now."

The cellular phone rang, startling the little girl, but quickly she closed her eyes again. Jeff answered it.

"Yeah?"

"You got the girl, mate?" It was Ben who spoke, and Jeff glanced at the child again.

"We've got her," he said with a slight smile. "Did you catch them?"

"No such luck. We waited till your van left the scene, and then we 'eaded over there. There wasn't a clue. The police 'ave been contacted now, though, and they're combing the area. Was the kid all right?"

"Scared out of her wits and wheezing a little, but other than that we can't see any physical damage. We're taking her home now. Will the doctor be there?"

"We'll call right now. We're on our way home."

Jeff hung up the phone, and looked at Leah. Her hair was tangled and stuck to her wet cheek, and tears still rolled down her face as she held the sleeping child. "He says they didn't have any luck finding the kidnappers. The police have been called in now. Your father and the others are on their way to your house."

Leah nodded, but for a moment, she didn't speak. "What if they come back?" she whispered finally. "What if they think it was so easy that they try it again? I can't believe they're still out there...."

As he drove the rest of the way to her home, Jeff couldn't find an answer to calm her fears.

CONTROLLED CHAOS ABOUNDED around Leah's house as they pulled into her driveway. Three police cars and an ambulance waited on the street, their lights flashing and radios blaring. Neighbors had come out of the condos across the street wearing robes and slippers and had clustered in the street, watching.

"What the hell . . . ?" Jeff threw a helpless look to Leah. "Your father doesn't waste any time, does he?"

Leah tightened her hold on the sleeping, wheezing child. "Jeff, I don't want them frightening her. I want her to have some peace—"

Someone knocked on the window, and he looked out into the blaring light of a television camera. "Damn. Can you open the garage? I can pull in—"

A police officer knocked on Leah's window, but ignoring him, Leah reached for the remote control garage door opener on the sun visor and brought the door up.

"They're following us in!" Leah said.

"Just answer their questions and we can get this over with," he said. "We want them to find the kidnappers."

He bent over her and opened her door and reached for the duffel bag as she slipped out, still holding Casey.

"How is she, Miss Borgadeux?"

"We have an ambulance waiting...."

"Are you all right?"

"Did you find them?" Leah asked one of the officers. "Did you catch the kidnappers?"

"Not yet, ma'am. We need to ask you a few questions."

"Miss Borgadeux!"

She glanced aside at a familiar reporter who had stuck a microphone in her face. "Did you see the kidnappers?"

"No," she said, shielding Casey's eyes from the light. "Excuse me. I have to get her in—"

"Is she all right? Did they harm her?"

"She seems fine," she said. "But you're waking her up. Please—"

Jeff broke through the crowd as Casey lifted her head and began to cry.

"Get a close-up," the reporter instructed his cameraman. Jeff took Leah's shoulders and began guiding her to the door.

The child screamed louder as the crowd pressed in, and she blinked at the television lights and railed an octave higher. "Damn it, turn that thing off!" Jeff shouted.

"Miss Borgadeux how much ransom was involved?"

Jeff held a hand in front of the camera. "She's going in now, pal!" He found her house key on the key chain and opened the door. The reporter started to follow them in, but Jeff blocked the entrance. "Nobody's coming in here except for one cop and the doctor. No reporters, and that means you."

"And who are you?" the reporter asked, pointing the mike at Jeff.

He started to say he was Casey's father, but reality hit, and he realized that his family would hear it over the news before he had the chance to tell them himself. "A friend of the family," he said finally. "Now get the hell out of here."

Borgy's Jaguar pulled into the driveway, effectively luring the reporters away, and Jeff let the cop in and closed the door.

Leah took Casey into the living room and, sitting down, tried to comfort her. As Casey's cries weakened, Leah's own tears intensified. She closed her eyes and squeezed them tightly shut as she buried her face in the child's hair.

In the light of the living room Jeff got his first good look at the little girl who was his daughter. Mesmerized, he was helpless to do anything more than stare.

"Did you see the car, Mr. Hampton?" the officer who'd come in with them asked.

"No. We didn't see anything."

The radio on his hip blared static police calls, and Jeff had the sudden urge to rip it off the cop's belt and throw it as far as he could. "Was the voice familiar? Could you identify—"

The door burst open, and Borgadeux and his detectives spilled inside, bringing with them two more cops and the television crew.

"I told them to stay out," Jeff said. "Where the hell is that doctor?"

"Here," one of the last men to come in called. Jeff looked down at the man's black bag and parted the crowd for him.

"How's Casey?" the doctor asked, instantly making Jeff feel as if he knew her.

"She's upset," he said.

"Any wheezing?"

Jeff led him into the living room. "Yes. And this damned mob isn't helping matters any."

The doctor took a look at the frightened child, still crying in her mother's arms.

"Thanks for coming, Dr. Marks," Leah said over the cries. "See, Casey? It's just Dr. Marks."

The doctor saw the extent of Casey's despair and turned around to the crowd coming in behind him.

"All right, let's clear this room. She needs quiet, and I can't examine her properly with all this commotion."

"Everybody out!" Borgadeux's powerful voice boomed over the chaos. "We'll be out with a statement later. Come on. Everybody except the doctor and the police officers."

Jeff refrained from pointing out that over half the crowd still remained, but he left it up to the tycoon to get them out. Going back to Leah's side, he watched as the doctor slipped off Casey's clothes, talking gently as he worked, examining her for any sign of harm despite her weary whimpers.

Too nervous to sit still, he pushed past the cops waiting their turn and went into Casey's room to get the air compressor he had seen earlier, to set up the nebulizer for the child's breathing treatment. Bringing it back into the living room, he plugged it in. "Where do you keep the mask and nebulizer?" he asked softly.

"In the kitchen. Second cabinet on the right."

He went in and found the necessary pieces in a sterile bag, tore it open and grabbed the three medicine bottles and vial of saline, and brought them back to Leah.

She took them with her free hand. "Thank you, Jeff."

He stooped down next to them and watched the doctor listening to Casey's breathing. "I didn't know which medicines you needed, so I brought them all."

She pointed to the ones she needed, and instructed him on how to mix them. In seconds, she slipped the mask over Casey's pale face and turned on the machine. A fine therapeutic mist floated out of the airholes on the mask.

"Is she okay, Dr.?"

The doctor smiled, and Jeff decided at once that he liked him. Leah had made a good choice in pediatricians.

"She'll be just fine as soon as we get this wheezing under control," he said. "Everything else looks fine. They must have handled her with care. She's a very lucky little girl."

"Yeah, right."

He watched as Casey tried to shove her thumb through the air hole in the mask and put it in her mouth. Closing her eyes tightly, she relaxed against Leah and tried to sleep.

The cops sat down, their hip radios still blaring, and Borgy and his detectives came in.

"Did you see anyone at all at the park?" the cop began to ask. "Any parked cars? Anyone sitting on a bench, standing in the shadows?"

"Nobody," Jeff said. "It was dead quiet." He looked at Casey, falling asleep against Leah, still wearing the mask as if it was a familiar routine.

"Me and my men can give you all the details you need, mate," Ben told the cop. "We 'ave recordings in the kitchen as well as the note."

Two of the cops followed him out. The third one gave them a tentative look. "You know, it wouldn't hurt to talk to the reporters. Since the kidnappers haven't been apprehended, maybe someone who hears about it might have some information. Besides, they're going to report it whether you talk to them or not. You want them to get the facts straight."

"Dad can talk to them," Leah said, her voice flat. "He can tell them everything they want to know. I just... I just can't right now."

A flurry of activity followed in the kitchen, but Jeff stayed in the living room, his eyes never leaving the tiny child clinging in her sleep to her three favorite things—her bunny, her blankie and her mother—while she breathed the vaporized mist into her lungs. That he wasn't among those favorite things ate at him from the core of his being, and he felt his anger being crowded out by sheer despair.

An hour later, after he'd finished with the reporters outside, Lance Borgadeux ambled into the room, putting himself between Jeff and Leah. "Fumbling idiots let them get away," he said. "They're still out there. It was so easy for them. They'll try it again, you know."

Jeff saw the terror seeping back into Leah's weary eyes.

"I want you to come home with me...tonight," he said. "Right now. You and Casey will be safe there, Leah."

Jeff saw her drop her face into the child's soft curls, and he could see that she struggled with the decision.

"You can't stay here," Borgadeux said. "You'll be all alone... vulnerable...."

"I'll stay with her."

Jeff's words sounded so foreign to him, that for a moment he wasn't aware that he had uttered them.

Borgy turned around, regarded him with a threatening look, and Leah looked up at him.

"I'll stay here," he repeated. "I won't leave her. She'll be safe."

Borgadeux came to his feet, his big form lacking the intimidation it once held for Jeff. "Who the hell do you think you are?"

"I think I'm the child's father," Jeff said, giving him a what-are-you-gonna-do-about-it look. "And if anybody's going to protect them, it's going to be me."

"And you think you can hold off dangerous criminals trying to get at my granddaughter?"

"Yeah, I think I can."

"And what if you're wrong, hotshot? What if you can't?"

"And what if *you* can't?" Jeff shot back.

"I live in a mansion," the tycoon said. "I have guards at the gates, guards at the doors, guards inside the house, security systems that alert the police at the drop of a paper clip, close-circuit televisions that pan the grounds. Just what do you have to offer her?"

"I care," Jeff said. "I care about what happens to that little girl, and by God, I'm not going to sit here and let you bully Leah into hiding her away from me now that I know about her. Not unless it's what she wants."

The qualifier seemed to please Borgadeux, and smiling, he turned back to his daughter. "Tell him, Leah. Tell him where you'd rather be."

Leah's voice was hoarse when she spoke. "I'll stay here, Daddy," she whispered. "If Jeff will stay with us, I'll stay here."

"Are you out of your mind? Do you know what kind of danger you're putting yourself and that child in?"

Confusion settled over Leah's eyes, and she turned them back to Jeff. Despair clouded over her expression, once again, as she kissed the top of Casey's head. "Maybe he's right, Jeff. We don't really know what we're dealing with."

"I can take care of you and Casey until the kidnappers are caught," he said without a doubt. "You owe this to me, Leah. You owe me the chance to do that."

"This isn't about owing," Leah whispered.

"No, Leah," he said. "It's about trusting. As far as I can see, nobody here really trusts anybody."

"I trust you," she whispered.

But I don't trust you, he thought. If she took the child to her father's and he locked them away there, Jeff's chances of seeing Casey again were next to nothing. And he didn't trust Leah to care about that one way or another.

"Then stay here," he told her. "Stay here with me."

The words, uttered so confidently, washed over her with warm security. Security that she hadn't known in such a long time. It was nice to have someone to take care of her, someone to worry about her, someone to take part of the burden off her shoulders.

Someone besides her father, who only added new ones when he took the old ones away.

The medicine ran out, and Leah removed Casey's mask and cut off the machine. "I'm staying here, Dad," she whispered, coming to her feet with the baby asleep in her arms. "I think it's best for Casey to sleep in her own bed tonight. If she wakes up in the middle of the night, I want her to know where she is. I don't want her to have to be afraid again." Not waiting for a reply, she headed toward her daughter's room.

Borgadeux swung around to the man who'd come between his daughter and him once before. "I'm warning you, Hampton, you'll regret the day you ever crossed me if you keep getting in my way."

"Funny," Jeff said. "I was just about to say the exact same thing."

"She doesn't want you," he said. "She made that clear two and a half years ago. She dumped you, then had your baby and didn't even tell you. Does that sound like a woman who wants you around?"

He couldn't deny that it didn't, but at this point, that wasn't the issue. "I don't care if she wants me around or not," Jeff said honestly. "The point is that I'm going to protect my daughter, I'm going to get to know her and I'm going to let her know that she has a father she can count on. And I don't give a rat's ass what you or your daughter think about it."

Borgadeux gave a frustrated, sarcastic, even threatening chuckle and shook his head. "You don't know what you're getting into, Hampton. This isn't wise."

"Your threats don't work on me anymore, Borgy. I'm immune."

"Nobody's immune," Borgadeux said, his eyes suddenly deadly serious. "I don't think you understand how far I'm willing to go for my daughter and grandchild's sake."

Jeff met his eyes with seething seriousness of his own. "And I don't think you understand how far I'm willing to go. This child casts a whole new light on the subject, Borgy. She's my flesh and blood . . . my family. And if you have any delusions that I'm going to disappear, think again. I can fight just as dirty as you can.''

He saw Borgy's eyes dart to the bedroom door and turned to see Leah standing in the doorway. He wasn't sure how much she'd heard, but from the look on her face, he knew she'd heard enough.

"She's sleeping," Leah whispered.

Her hair was wild and tousled around her face, and she didn't wear a stitch of makeup. To look at her, one would never know that she was the pampered princess of the Borgadeux fortune. One would think she had character, and warmth and heart.

"Are the police gone?"

Borgadeux nodded. "They said they'd keep us informed. Ben and Willy and Jack left with the cops."

"And the reporters?"

Borgadeux shrugged. "I'll give them what they want in a minute."

Leah nodded silently. "I'm really tired, Daddy. I'd like to get some sleep."

Borgy looked back at Jeff, his eyes still threatening. "Leah, you have to—"

From the bedroom, Casey started to cry, and Leah turned and fled from the room.

"Give it up, Borgy," Jeff said.

Cursing under his breath, Borgy grabbed up his keys from the counter and slammed out of the house.

JEFF WAITED A MOMENT, staring at the closed door, listening to the quiet of the house, breathing the scent of Leah's turf. They were alone. Finally. And just in there, just beyond the hallway, was his little girl. Safe and sound.

She had stopped crying when Leah had gone to her, and quietly he stepped into the darkened hallway and to the door of Casey's room. Leah was sitting on the edge of the bed, holding her, and Casey's eyes were closed again.

"Is she all right?" he whispered, not wanting to disturb her.

Leah looked up at him, saw the apprehension in his eyes, the reluctance to step into the circle of love the little girl wore about her. She smiled and nodded. "She's fine. She just woke up and got scared."

He lingered at the doorway, as if he had no right to come farther into the room, now that the child was back.

"Thank you for staying," Leah whispered. "I really didn't want to go back with my father."

He didn't answer. Instead, his eyes fell from Leah's eyes to the child, whose head was relaxing back on Leah's arm.

"Is he gone?"

Jeff looked up at her. "Who?"

"My father. Is he gone yet?"

"Yeah," Jeff said.

"How'd you do it?" she asked softly. "Make him leave, I mean."

He shrugged. "Just let him know I couldn't be pushed around."

Realizing that the conversation wasn't about to be two-way, Leah hushed and looked down at the child in her arms. Casey's breathing had relaxed to a steady cadence, free of wheezing, and her thumb had fallen out of her mouth.

"You can sleep in my bed tonight," she whispered.

His eyes darted up to hers, and Leah blushed... something that surprised him, for in the last two and a half years, he had tried hard to forget those little vulnerabilities about her. Instead, he'd concentrated on her coldness, her selfishness, her unyieldingness on the day she had left him.

"I mean... I'm going to sleep in here with Casey. I don't want her to be alone."

"Fine."

She looked up from the child and settled her eyes on him again. It seemed that they were strangers, with nothing in common except the child. The child he didn't even know.

Quiet grew like a wall between them, defining the darkness of the voids in both their lives.

Finally, Jeff pushed away from the door's casing and started to walk away.

"Jeff?"

He stopped in the hallway, turned back.

"Would you like to hold her for a minute before I put her down?"

He froze, but despite his seeming paralysis, his heart accelerated. "Won't she...won't she wake up? Won't it scare her?"

"She's sleeping pretty soundly," she whispered. "I think it'll be all right. Besides, I'll be right here."

For a moment, he didn't make a move to come nearer. He only stood at the doorway, staring at the child, with eyes that held the slightest trace of terror.

Finally, he took a step toward her.

Leah stood up and met him across the room. For a moment they looked at each other, that trust that he had sworn to be so lacking in her radiating like candlelight in her eyes. She trusted him enough to hand over her child. Even if it was for only a moment.

Taking a deep breath and trapping it in his lungs, he opened his arms and allowed her to place the child in them.

She was light, he thought as a soft, poignant, yet sad smile came to his lips. And sweet. And warm.

Quietly, he backed to the rocking chair and lowered himself into it. Distributing her weight across his lap and pulling her closer, he looked down at her little face, which he hadn't had the chance to really see clearly since it had been hidden behind a thumb or crushed against her mother's breast ever since they'd found her.

Her face was shaped like his, he thought, long and narrow, and her little nose reminded him of his own baby pictures. But her mouth was Leah's—soft and full and pouting....

His heart burst at the sight and feel of the child in his arms, and slowly he bent down and pressed a kiss on her forehead.

Leah came closer, knelt beside him and smiled softly at the delicate gesture. She saw the tears mist over in his eyes. Saw the way his throat convulsed. Saw how his hands trembled.

Gently, she set a reassuring hand on his knee, letting him know that he was doing everything right.

The edges of his mouth trembled as he dropped his face down into Casey's curls, just like he had seen Leah do a hundred times since they'd been home. She smelled of baby shampoo and Leah, and suddenly, the sensation of loss welled so deeply inside him that he couldn't fight the feeling breaking out over his face.

Leah saw it, and the pain he struggled with found its own seat in her heart. "What is it, Jeff?" she whispered, desperate to help him with the burden of his pain, as he had helped her tonight. "What are you thinking?"

His lips tightened across his teeth as he brought his moist eyes to hers. "I was thinking," he whispered, "that I don't know how I'll ever forgive you for what you've done to me."

Chapter Six

In Leah's face, Jeff saw the pain his words had inflicted, but he told himself she deserved to hurt. He had every right to hate her.

And yet, there was Casey, lying asleep between them, curled snug and warm in his arms. The one bond that would unite them for the rest of their lives, despite all that had passed before.

"I can't blame you for that," she managed to say after a moment. "And for what it's worth, I never expected you to forgive me."

His eyes fell from Leah back to the little girl in his arms. He wondered how much she had weighed at birth, if she would have fit perfectly from the palm of his hand to the crook of his elbow, if he would have been able to burp her, feed her, diaper her. He wondered if Leah had breast-fed.

Idly, his eyes strayed to the woman kneeling in front of him, and slowly, pensively, dropped to her breasts, covered by cotton fabric. Tearing his eyes away, he began to rock as the child felt more comfortable in his arms.

Her curls spilled down his bare arm, and he wondered if she'd been born with a lot of hair, and if it had been curly at birth. He wondered if she'd slept all night at first, how old she'd been when she'd said her first word.

Again, his eyes drifted to Leah's small body, a body that had always made him feel so strong, so protective. And so miserable.

It was Leah's soft, sad voice that finally broke the quiet. "It's late," she whispered. "We should get some sleep."

Jeff nodded and looked down at the sleeping child, but he didn't want to let her go. If he could feel this way in one night, he thought, how intense must Leah's feelings for the child be after two years?

She stood up and pulled back the covers on Casey's bed. Slowly, Jeff came to his feet and laid the child on her side, repositioning the blanket against her face and the bunny near her hand, where she wouldn't have to look far to find them.

Leah watched as he remained bent over her, stroked the hair back from her face, pulled up the covers and pressed a soft, undisturbing kiss on her temple. He turned back to Leah, raked his hand through his hair and avoided her eyes. "Do you need anything from your room before I go to bed?"

She shook her head. "No, nothing."

He started for the door, but she reached out and caught his arm. "Jeff?"

Not looking back, he stopped.

"Thank you," she whispered. "I couldn't have gotten through this without you."

Jeff turned around and gave her a cold, heartless look. "You owe me, Leah. And I intend to collect."

"You will," she whispered. Leah waited until he was out of sight, until she heard her bedroom door close, before she pulled back Casey's covers and lay down beside the child. It didn't matter that she was still dressed. All that mattered was that Casey was back in her arms. And Jeff was here, too.

She dropped her head on the pillow, which Casey rarely used, and tried not to think about the shower that she heard running, or the fact that Jeff had opted to spend the night with her to protect her. It wasn't her safety he cared about, she told herself, but Casey's. And that was all right. That was enough.

The clock ticked on, until she heard the water cut off, heard the mattress of her bed squeak beneath his weight. She wondered if his hair was wet, what that day's growth of stubble felt like on his jaw, if her soap smelled differently on him than it did on her.

And then she told herself to stop wondering. It was no use. She had destroyed any possibility she'd ever had of resuming things with him.

But even knowing that, it felt wonderful to know he was there, in the next room, watching over her. Even if he could never love her again, she was glad to have him back in her life.

IT WAS HOURS LATER when Jeff gave up the idea of sleeping. How could he be expected to lie in Leah's house, in Leah's bed, between her sheets, on her pillow, and not think of her? The scent of her hair and her skin brought back a flood tide of memories that he lacked the energy to fight. Memories of their driving off to Sanibel Island on the spur of the moment, of their pitching a tent on the beach and making love with the autumn breeze sweeping across their skin.

Was that when they had conceived Casey? Or had it been the Christmas weekend they'd spent in his apartment, making tree ornaments out of popcorn, glue and glitter, painting the windows with artificial snow? Had it been before or after he'd given her the small diamond necklace he'd shopped for weeks for— the one that matched the ring he had planned to give her later?

The one she hadn't accepted.

Pulling out of bed, he went to the window, and looked out onto the Gulf lapping against the shore behind her house. The moonlight defined the white-caps ruffling the water, and he thought there was going to be another storm soon.

Restless, he walked around her bedroom, taking in the personal items that he didn't want to see, for he had no interest in knowing any more about her than the fact that she'd stepped on his heart and betrayed him in the deepest way.

He picked up her brush, saw flaxen hairs threaded through, and remembered the time he had brushed and braided her hair, that night on Sanibel Island. It felt like silken threads slipping through his fingers, without a tangle, without a kink. It was baby hair, he'd told her, and she had laughed.

He set the brush down and went to the picture of her and Casey framed and angled on the dresser. Casey was laughing, and Leah smiled with the most serene smile he'd seen on her. Had motherhood really changed her? Had it taken the restlessness from her spirit? The insecurity that her father had spent her whole life instilling?

Idly, he went from the dresser to her chest of drawers, and saw the little jewelry box lying on top. Knowing he shouldn't, he opened it. The diamond necklace he had given her was tucked in a satin pocket, and he pulled it out, held it in his palm. Did she wear it? Or did she keep it hidden away, like the ring he hadn't even looked at since he'd sworn to put her out of his heart.

You could sell it and get all that money back, Jan had told him more than once. *It must have cost a fortune.*

But Jan had never understood that, when he bought it for Leah, she had been *worth* a fortune to him. He just hadn't been worth that much to her. He kept it as a reminder not to make the same mistake again—not to trust that fickle, fatal emotion poets called love for want of any more accurate, more scathing word.

He heard a humming within the house and, instantly more alert, opened the door quietly and looked out. He realized the sound was coming from Casey's room.

Slowly, he made his way through the darkness to her door, and saw the source of the noise sitting on a towel in the corner of the room. It was the humidifier, blowing a fine mist of cool air throughout the room, making Casey's breathing come easier. He wondered how long ago Leah had filled it with water and turned it off.

He looked at the bed, saw Leah was sound asleep, her arms firmly around her child—his child—just as Casey's arms were firmly holding her blankie and bunny. Leah's hair was splayed across the pillow, and her mouth was slightly open, making her look innocent and pure rather than selfish and conniving.

He turned away.

He had watched her sleep many times before, and always, it had melted his heart. Like the child, she was beautiful.

But she was also dangerous.

She stirred slightly, and he saw her shiver. The covers had fallen off her in favor of the child, and he realized that the temperature had dropped. Looking around, he saw the afghan lying on the trunk in the corner of the room. He picked it up, feeling the soft knit of it, and laid it gently over her.

Quickly, he backed out of the room, desperate to put some distance between them. This wasn't going to be easy, he told himself, but he was doing it for his child, not for Leah. He wasn't going to let his feelings about her spoil his new relationship with his daughter. Nothing would keep him from knowing Casey, or from letting her know him.

More tired now than he had been before, he went back to Leah's room, climbed once again into her bed and laid his head on her pillow. Wrapped in the scent and softness of her possessions, he slept.

"I WANT GUMMI BEARS."

Casey's first words, at 7:00 a.m. the next morning, brought Leah instantly awake. The child was sitting up in bed. A tuft of curls fell over her face, and her eyes were still sleepy. She looked the way she did on any average morning. Healthy, happy, and here...right here where Leah could reach up and kiss her warm little cheek.

"Good morning, sweetheart."

"Gummi Bears, Mommy. Turn on the TV."

Leah's smile blossomed to a full flower, and she sat up and hugged Casey. "You got it, pumpkin. Come on. I'll race you to the TV."

Giggling, Casey hopped off the bed and, dragging her blanket behind her and still clutching her bunny's ear, she ran as fast as her plump little legs would carry her.

Leah reached the television seconds after Casey. "You won!" She raised Casey's fist in mock victory. "Even with a ten-pound diaper—" she said, patting the wet diaper dropping to the child's knees "—you still beat me."

Casey giggled and poked the power button on the television, where the Gummi Bears cartoon sprang to life. Then, ignoring the wet diaper, the child climbed up onto the couch, put her thumb in her mouth and began watching.

"You little rascal," Leah said, sitting down next to her and smoothing her hair. "You'd think it was any other morning." *Not the morning after you were kidnapped.*

Tears came to her eyes, and she smeared them away before her daughter could see them. "So are you hungry?"

Casey nodded. "I want a Tootsie Pop and five do-nuts," she said, holding up two fingers.

"No can do," Leah said with a smirk. "How about oatmeal, yogurt or cereal?"

"No can do," Casey said.

"All right then. How about eggs and bacon?"

"How 'bout cupcakes?"

"You mean *pan*cakes?"

"With syrup?"

Feeling as if she'd been outsmarted, Leah messed up the child's hair and planted a kiss on her neck, sending Casey into a delightful round of giggles. "All right, you little con artist. Pancakes with syrup. This morning you could probably talk Mommy into anything. But first, let's get you out of this diaper."

Casey's smile faded as her eyes focused on something in the door, and Leah turned around to see Jeff standing there, wearing only his jeans. His chest was bare, except for the sprinkles of hair curling across it, hair she had flirted with and splayed her hands through. His eyes were sleepy, and his hair was mussed.

She thought he had never looked better.

"Hi," she said with a smile.

"Hi." His greeting was soft, tentative and more directed at the child than her.

Casey's thumb headed for her mouth.

Leah smiled again. "She's in a good mood. Like nothing ever happened."

"That's a good sign. Isn't it?"

"I think so," she said. She turned back to Casey. "What do you think, squirt?"

"I think cupcakes," Casey said, looking up at Jeff with eyes the size of quarters, apprehensive eyes that seemed to fear his presence as though it meant she wasn't going to get those pancakes.

"Pancakes," Leah corrected.

"With syrup."

It was Jeff's turn to smile.

Leah picked Casey up, put her on her lap and pointed up to Jeff. "Casey, do you remember who this is?"

Casey was silent for a long moment as she studied the strange man who had come from her mother's bedroom, wearing only a pair of jeans. Her thumb gravitated to her mouth.

"He's Jeff," Leah prompted. "And he's..." She met Jeff's eyes, swallowed. "He's your daddy. Can you say 'daddy'?"

She saw the poignant expression on Jeff's face, but Casey shook her head.

Jeff stooped in front of her. "That's okay. She doesn't have to call me that yet. She can call me Jeff."

"Daddy's as easy to learn as Jeff," Leah said. "Isn't it, Casey?"

Casey took the thumb from her mouth, and cocked her head at Jeff. They held their breath, waited.

"You want cupcakes?" she asked.

Jeff grinned. "You feed her cupcakes for break-fast?"

Leah rolled her eyes. "*Pan*cakes."

"With syrup," Casey added.

And as they all started for the kitchen, Leah wondered how long this feeling of pure, unadulterated happiness could last.

THE ANSWER CAME LATER that morning, when Casey sat at her little play table smashing clay pancakes, and Leah and Jeff finally found themselves alone in the kitchen.

"We have a lot to take care of today."

Leah turned around at the sink and saw Jeff rubbing his tired eyes and looking at her.

"Like what?" she asked.

"Like seeing to it that those kidnappers are caught. Plus, I would really like to introduce Casey to my sister and call my parents. They should be told about her." He breathed a dry laugh and brought his coffee to his mouth. "I can just hear it now. 'Hey, Mom, I just thought I'd give you a call and let you know that you have a two-year-old granddaughter. Why didn't I tell you? Well, because the mother forgot to tell me.'"

Leah dropped a pan in the sink and felt her face growing hot. "I didn't forget and you know it."

"No, you didn't forget," he said. "But that's infinitely easier to explain than the real reason."

She dried her hands roughly on a towel and turned back to him. "Look, Jeff, nobody would blame you if you just picked up and walked out of here right now. I can take care of myself and my daughter—"

"*Our* daughter," he corrected. "And you'd like that, wouldn't you? For me to just disappear again?"

"No," she said, emotion quivering on her voice. "As a matter of fact, I wouldn't. Believe it or not, I'm glad you're here."

"Yeah, right." He pushed back his chair and stood up. "Anyway, I won't leave you and Casey alone today...not while those kidnappers are still on the loose. You'll have to come with me."

Leah nodded. "I didn't plan on opening the shop today, anyway. All the publicity—"

"You mentioned that earlier," he said. "What is it you do?"

"I have a dress shop," she said. "It's called Leah's, and it's how I support Casey and me."

"Oh," he said. "I thought—"

"That I was living off of my father? I told you I wasn't. I opened the shop with a small business loan I got on my own. It hasn't been easy, either, but I've managed."

He looked at her pensively for a moment. "What do you know? You an entrepreneur...."

"And a good one," she said. "But since I'm not opening today, Casey and I can go with you to your work site. I'd like to see what you're working on."

Her interest surprised him, but he pretended to ignore it. "Before that, we'll drop by the office of a private investigator I know, get him started on the case—"

"But my father's people are working on it. And the police—"

"And they haven't found them yet," he cut in. "It can't hurt to have one more person on it."

"I guess not." Leah stepped toward him, a frown wrinkling her brow. She didn't have on a stitch of makeup, and her hair had yet to be brushed. He couldn't remember ever seeing her look so tousled ... even after the night they'd spent on the beach, she had slipped away and put on a touch of makeup before he could see her the next morning.

But oddly enough, she had never appeared more beautiful to him. That thought made him angry.

"Jan will be at my work site, so I can take care of a few things while we're there."

Leah took a dishrag to the table and began to wipe away the breakfast spills. "Jan probably doesn't have real good feelings about me."

"Nope, she doesn't," he said in a you-made-your-bed-now-sleep-in-it tone. "And after this, she'll downright hate you. But hey, that's the breaks."

His nonchalant way of dealing with his pain made hers even more pronounced, and she shoved her hair back from her face. "Look, Jeff, I'm not fighting you on any of this. I'm grateful for your being here, whether I deserve it or not. I'm grateful for your attitude toward Casey, and I'm grateful for your protection and concern for her. But in order for both of us to tolerate this situation, you've got to stop sniping at me. Casey will sense it, and it won't do either of us any good."

Jeff looked through the doorway to Casey, who had begun making "beans" out of her clay. As she played, she hummed bits and pieces of "Itsy Bitsy Spider." The sight of her softened his lips.

"Do you think she remembers yesterday at all?"

"Of course." Leah sighed and went to stand beside him in the doorway. "I'm just hoping that her attitude today means that she wasn't traumatized too badly. Maybe they were nice to her."

"The police said she needs to see a psychologist for evaluation."

"Yeah," she whispered. "I'm not looking forward to it."

"I'll come with you," he said quietly.

She nodded, wondering how he could be sarcastic and angry one minute, then sweet and considerate the next. It frightened and confused her.

"So...do you want the bathroom first?"

She smiled. "If it's okay. Sorry there's only one."

He shrugged. "That's all right. I have a hot date for some clay pancakes with a cute little two-year-old I know." As he spoke, he went and sat down beside Casey, and she started to giggle.

For the moment, Casey was too distracted by the man molding teddy bears out of her clay to notice that her mother had left them alone. But the moment Leah turned the shower on, the child looked around for her mother.

"Where's Mommy?"

"She's taking a shower," Jeff said, handing her the molded teddy bear.

Casey stood up, knocking over her little chair. "I want my mommy."

"Take it easy," Jeff said quietly. "She's just in there."

Tears burst to Casey's eyes, and she ran to the bathroom door. "Mommy!"

"Wait. Mommy'll be right out."

The child's cries rose to high-pitched, terrified screams. "No! I want my mommy! I want my mommy now!"

Throwing herself against the door, Casey reached for the doorknob, turned it. The door opened, and a thick cloud of steam rolled out, its fragrant scent wafting over the house. "Mommy! Mommy!"

The water was cut off. "Mommy's here, honey. What's wrong? What is it? Jeff!"

Jeff stopped in the doorway, trying not to look toward the drawn curtain. "I'm here, Leah. She got spooked when she noticed you were gone."

The child's screams grew more panicked, and she tried to scale the bathtub to get in with Leah. Her foot slipped, sending Casey sprawling backward on the wet floor. A bloodcurdling scream tore from her throat.

Forgetting why he couldn't go in, Jeff burst into the bathroom and snatched her up.

Leah held the thin plastic curtain against her and looked out the side of it. "Is she all right?"

"No harm done," he said over the child's screams. "She didn't hit her head." He sat down on the lid of the toilet, struggling to calm her.

He looked up and saw the silhouette of Leah's bare body behind the curtain, the shampoo dripping from her hair, the water beading on her naked shoulder. His throat went dry and he stood up and started back for the door. "Come on, Casey. We'll wait for Mommy outside the door, okay?"

"No!" Squirming to get down, Casey screamed again, the sound breaking Leah's heart. "Mommy!"

Quickly, Leah turned the water back on. "Just let Mommy rinse out her hair, okay, baby?"

Jeff turned his back to the shower. "Leah, if I let her down, she's going to slip again. And I don't want to upset her by taking her back out."

"Then stay here."

He glanced over his shoulder. "What?"

"Just sit in here with her. She'll calm down if she realizes you aren't trying to take her. I'm hurrying."

Not knowing if her idea was such a good one, he readjusted the squirming, crying girl on his hip and sat again on the lid of the toilet. "Okay, Casey. We're going to sit right here and wait for Mommy, okay? You can see her right through that curtain. See?" As the child calmed, his own heartbeat accelerated. His voice, however, retained its soothing, honey tone. "Mommy's not going to leave you, and nobody's going to take you from her. Okay?"

Still hiccuping her sobs, the child rubbed at her eyes and laid her head back on his chest. "Be-cos I want my mommy," she whimpered.

"I know you do." His eyes strayed to the silhouette behind the curtain as Leah arched her back and rinsed out her hair. Her breasts were fuller than he remembered and her hips smaller. He wondered how it would feel to step into the shower with her and lather those soft, delicate curves, and feel her body against his just one more time.

She cut off the shower.

"Uh . . . could you hand me the towel?" Her voice sounded awkward, tense.

He lifted the towel off of its rod and handed it to her, keeping his head turned.

"I'm really sorry about this," she said from behind the curtain. Despite his efforts to keep his eyes diverted, his gaze gravitated to the naked shadow as she towel-dried her body. His mouth went dry as she moved the towel over her breasts, her arms, her flat stomach, her legs.... "Having a two-year-old can be pretty demanding."

Vaguely, he picked up the thread of her words. His voice sounded distant and distracted when he answered. "I can handle it," he said absently.

He watched her silhouette wrap the towel around her, watched her tuck a corner between her breasts. Slowly, self-consciously, she pulled the curtain back slightly. "I guess this insecurity answers our question about her remembering yesterday."

There was still a cluster of wet drops on her shoulder, and he fought the urge to smooth them away with his fingers. "Yeah."

She noted the clipped way he spoke and the way his throat convulsed as he looked at her. "You could probably set her down now. I can take it from here."

"Yeah." He felt silly, only uttering monosyllables, but he was afraid his voice would give him away if he tried to say more. He set Casey down and stood up.

"I'm sorry about all that. You should be able to take a shower without an audience."

Leah smiled. "You obviously have a lot to learn about parenthood. I haven't taken a shower alone in two years."

He turned back and gave her a soft smile, and of their own accord, his eyes fell to those bare, wet shoulders again, to the swell of her breasts, to the bare, thin legs and the wet feet with apricot-colored toenails.

As if she didn't notice his pensive scrutiny of her, she bent over to her daughter. "You okay now, Casey? You know Mommy's not going to leave you?"

Casey stuck her thumb in her mouth and nodded as Jeff closed the door behind him.

MOMENTS LATER, when Leah dressed and turned the bathroom over to him, he didn't even try to use the hot water. Cold, icy jets sprayed over him, but it did nothing to ease the physical ache produced by what he had seen earlier.

He tried to block out the memory of her body sliding over his so long ago. Tried to forget the honey-sweet taste of her mouth as she'd responded so completely to him.

When he came out, freshly shaven with the razor she'd left for him, he found them both sitting in the living room waiting for him. All remnants of Casey's tears were gone, and she was dressed in a frilly little sundress. Her hair, long ringlets to her shoulders, was pulled back from her face with a big white bow.

He smiled and stooped in front of Casey. "I think you might just look pretty enough to deserve a Tootsie Pop."

Casey's eyes lit up. "I want a red one."

"One red Tootsie Pop, coming up," he said. "We'll stop at the first store we come to."

Casey's smiled faded, and she gave Leah a troubled look. "Mommy come, too?"

Jeff glanced up at Leah. "Do I look like a man who would forget your mommy?"

The question, though meant innocently and flippantly, struck them both. Quickly, he rallied.

"Mommy's coming, too. You don't have to worry."

Demonstrating that she wasn't worried, Casey hopped down from the sofa beside her mother and headed for the bathroom. "Wanna see I'm big?"

He came to his feet. "Sure, I do."

"I can go potty."

Leah followed them back into the bathroom, noting that Jeff had dried the floor before he'd come out. "We've just embarked on the long road to potty training," she said as she tugged the little girl's training panties down.

She set Casey on the potty, and the child smiled up at them.

"You'd better get comfortable," Leah told Jeff. "This sometimes takes awhile."

Jeff stooped next to Casey. "I am just so profoundly amazed at how big you are," he said softly. "Up on the potty and everything."

"I'm big," she confirmed.

Promptly she slid off the toilet without having produced anything, and with her panties still at her ankles, reached over to flush. "See? All by myself."

Leah's smile matched his. "This is when we applaud."

The two began to cheer and clap as Casey struggled to get her panties back up. Continuing the jubilation,

Jeff swung her up off the floor, setting off a round of giggles. Slowly he lowered her to his face and set a kiss on her mouth.

Casey didn't object.

This must be what a family feels like, Leah thought as her laughter faded and fell into a soft smile. *Except that in a normal family, the father doesn't hate the mother.*

Quietly she started back out of the bathroom.

"Mommy!"

Leah turned around and saw the panicked look on Casey's face. "What, honey?"

"Don't leave me."

Exchanging looks with her, Jeff set her down and let the child scurry into her mother's arms.

"It's going to take some time," she said.

Jeff nodded. "I just happen to have a lot of that," he said. "Come on, let's go."

Chapter Seven

Together, they saw the psychologist, who evaluated Casey to the best of his ability and noted her fear of being separated from her mother again. Casey would have to learn how to trust, he told Leah. But that would take patience. It wouldn't happen overnight.

As they drove to the office of the private detective whom Jeff insisted on hiring to help in the search for the kidnappers, Leah thought of what the psychologist had said. Trust. It was something that Jeff was having trouble with, as well. And why should he trust her, after all? She had lied to him, hurt him, kept the most precious thing in his life from him....

She wondered what the good doctor might have to say about guilt, and self-forgiveness. She found it hard to believe that Jeff would ever be able to forgive her until the day she forgave herself. But that wasn't so easy.

Patience. She didn't know if she had enough, or if he did. Oh, it would be no problem to see Casey through her trauma. It would be no problem staying with her constantly until she was secure enough to be left again. It would be no problem letting Jeff into her child's life. What she wasn't sure of was whether or not she had the patience to wait for him to stop hating her.

They met with the private detective who bombarded them with new questions that she was happy to answer, praying all the while that he would be able to make headway where her father's people and the police had failed. The one time that she allowed him to question Casey, the child seemed to withdraw within herself and clung harder to Leah. Thankfully, Jeff had refused to let him ask Casey any more.

Casey conned Jeff out of a second Tootsie Pop sucker as they started to his work site to see Jan. Leah felt a new tension seeping into her bones. What must Jan think of her after what she'd done to Jeff? What would she think of her now, when she found out that her deceptions went much further than any of them had imagined.

If she'd had a choice, she would have stayed in the van. But Casey would never have gone in without her, so feeling like French royalty headed for the guillotine, she helped the child out of her car seat and started toward the trailer.

Jan was at the door before they had a chance to reach the trailer.

Instead of leaping on Jeff and chastising him for not telling her more, Jan crossed her arms and faced them squarely. "I saw the news this morning," she said, giving Jeff a guarded look and Leah a drop-dead one. Casey, she regarded with uncertainty.

"Hi, Jan," Leah whispered.

Ignoring her, Jan turned back to Jeff. "What's going on, Jeff?"

"Inside." He opened the door and motioned his sister in before him.

Reluctantly, Leah followed, carrying Casey, who still sucked on her Tootsie Pop and had a sticky pink ring around her mouth and coating her hands.

When they were inside the small trailer, Jan gave them all a sweeping look again. "Are you two back together or something?"

The question came with disapproval, sinking Leah's heart further. Jeff avoided her eyes.

"No," he said quickly. "Nothing like that. It's Casey." Reaching over to stroke her tendrils, he offered his sister a tentative smile. "Jan, Casey's my daughter."

Jan's face drained of all color, but from her expression, he knew she had already suspected after the news accounts on television. "Yours and . . . *hers?*"

"Yes." It was Leah who spoke this time.

"And you didn't tell me?"

"He didn't know," Leah said. "I kept it from him."

"You *what?*" As if the injustice had been directed solely at her, tears sprang to Jan's eyes. "You had my brother's child and didn't tell him?"

Jeff stepped between them. "Enough, Jan. We've been all through this, and now is not the time. For now, I wanted Casey to meet her aunt."

Slowly Leah set Casey down, and Jan's expression transformed into a sad, longing look as she bent over the child. "Aunt? I guess that does make me an aunt, huh?"

She stooped down, smiled at the candy on the child's face. "I see my brother's already spoiling you." Reaching for a tissue on her desk, she wiped the stickiness away then threw a look up at her brother. "Is she all right? I mean, after the kidnapping and all?"

Leah stooped next to Casey. "Yes. She's fine, except for being afraid to leave my side. They didn't hurt her. Not physically, anyway."

Jan gave Leah another cold look before turning her eyes back to Casey. "How old is she?"

"Two."

"Two." The word stuck in Jan's throat. "Two years you kept this from my brother?"

"Jan..." Jeff began, but Jan got to her feet.

"Jeff, can I see you outside for a minute, please?"

Jeff glanced awkwardly at Leah, then reluctantly at Casey. "Make yourselves at home," he said. "I'll only be a minute."

He followed Jan out of the trailer. When she reached the bottom of the steps she turned to face him, arms crossed. "Jeff, tell me that you aren't starting things back up with her. Instant family and all that."

"I told you I'm not. I'm just hanging around until the kidnappers are caught. Besides, I have a right to get to know my daughter."

"You're telling me! I hope you realize what kind of cruelty it takes for that woman to hide your child from you for the past two years. If she had ever known you, if she had ever loved you, she couldn't have done that. She would have known how much it would have meant to you."

"I'm well aware of that, Jan. And believe me, the last person in the world I want to get involved with is Leah Borgadeux. But she's the mother of my child. And right now, that's all that matters."

LEAH HEARD BITS and pieces of the conversation as it drifted through the open trailer window. She hadn't meant to listen, but there hadn't been a way to escape it.

The last person in the world I want to get involved with is Leah Borgadeux.

Jeff's words pierced at her heart, forcing a slow tear to trickle to her cheek. The funny thing was, she didn't blame him a bit.

How could a man who'd come from a loving home and a loving family ever understand the depths to which her father would have sunk to break them up? How could he ever understand that—at the time—she had believed she had no choices left?

But he couldn't, wouldn't ever understand that. It defied logic. The most she could hope for was that it wouldn't hinder his relationship with Casey. Or hers, later, when Casey grew up and learned what Leah had done.

Leaning over, she readjusted the bow in Casey's hair and pressed a kiss on her cheek. "Do you like your daddy?" she asked.

Casey nodded. "I like Tootsie Pops."

"That's all you're going to get for today, young lady." She wiped the tear off her face and lifted Casey into her lap.

The door opened, and Jeff came back in. Jan followed behind him. Offering Leah another cold look, she went around her desk. "Here are your messages," she said, handing a stack of notes to Jeff.

Jeff took them, flipped through. "I have to return a couple of these." He glanced at Leah. "Do you mind waiting a minute?"

"No, not at all." It was all so civil, she thought. The way they addressed each other over Casey's head, the way they pretended to get along.

He disappeared into his small office, and Jan went back to her desk and pretended to be absorbed in her work. But Leah wasn't fooled.

"Look, Jan..."

Jan held up a hand to stem Leah's words. "Don't. Whatever you're going to say, don't."

"I was just going to tell you that I don't blame you for disliking me. I'm not too pleased with myself right now."

Jan's sharp eyes met hers across the desk. "If you hurt him again, Leah, you're gonna pay for it. Somehow, you're gonna pay."

The words stung, and Leah thought of all the heartache she had suffered over the past two and a half years since she'd left him. It hadn't gone away, had only numbed into a manageable feeling that she'd grown used to. She thought of all the hard times she'd faced with Casey, times when she'd felt so lonely and so alone that she wondered how she would go on. She thought of all the men who had asked her out, men who by all rights should have held some attraction to her, but she'd turned them all away. And she thought of the constant, nagging memory of the man who possessed her heart, the man who now hated her. "I've already paid," she said.

The words seemed to make Jan angrier. "You've never paid for anything in your life."

Leah pulled Casey against her and gave Jan a look cool enough to match her own. "You don't know me," she said. "You don't know anything about me."

"I know enough."

The two women held each other's piercing gaze for a long moment, until a crash sounded behind Jan's desk. She swung around and saw a broken vase lying on the floor and a cat prowling away.

Casey gasped. "A catty! Mommy, look!"

The exclamation diverted their attention and brought the slightest hint of a smile to Jan's lips as she picked up the pieces of the vase. "He's a bad cat. He belongs to Jeff...I mean, your father...." She stooped to scoop up the cat and hold it out for Casey to pet. "What *does* she call him?"

"Nothing yet," Leah said softly. "But we're shooting for Daddy."

"Daddy." Jan repeated the word pensively as Casey reached out a tentative hand and touched the cat's soft fur. Her face resumed its tightness. "You know, I always looked forward to the day Jeff had a little one to wrap him around her finger, but I never expected it to happen like this."

"Neither did I," Leah whispered.

Jan tried to punch some life back into her smile as she looked at the child. "The cat's name is Sylvester, like in the cartoon. I think he likes you."

Casey giggled.

The cold edge to Jan's eyes died, and she touched Casey's curls. "She beautiful. She should be in commercials or something."

"Thank you." The words came softly, tentatively.

"She looks like him, doesn't she?"

Leah smiled. "I've always thought so."

They heard Jeff's footsteps across the trailer, and he came into the doorway and saw Casey petting the cat.

"Has Sylvester been sidling up to you?" he asked, bending over to Casey. "You have to be careful. He can get you into trouble sometimes."

As if in protest, the cat meowed.

Casey mewed back.

"Here," Jeff said, picking up Sylvester's ball off the floor, and handing it to Casey. "Throw this and he'll run after it."

Casey did as told, and the cat scurried after it, chasing the spongy ball as if it were a colorful little mouse. Casey slipped out of Leah's lap and followed the cat around the room.

"So..." Jeff said, looking from Leah to Jan. "What does Aunt Jan think of her niece?"

"I think that the minute you're out of here, I'm going to be on the phone looking for a talent agent. That kid belongs in the movies. We could put her picture on the front of a calendar and sell millions."

Smiling like a father, he stooped down and grabbed the ball. "Sorry, but I just found her. I'm not ready to share her yet."

Much to Sylvester's chagrin, he handed the ball to Casey, then messed up her curls. Jan looked at Leah again with an expression that warned she was watching her. Leah returned a look that said, *I know he's vulnerable right now. I won't take advantage of that.*

Jan went back to her desk and plopped into her chair. "The news said the kidnappers hadn't been caught. What are you going to do?"

The question was directed more to Jeff than to Leah, but Leah answered nonetheless.

"My father has a team of detectives on the case, the police are looking and today Jeff hired his own detective to look for them."

"Aren't you afraid?" she asked grudgingly.

"Yeah, a little." She glanced back at Jeff's strong shoulders as he bent over Casey, and thought how much more afraid she might be if she didn't have him.

"So when will you be back at work?" Jan asked her brother.

"I don't know. I'll let you know."

He leaned over, put his hands under Casey's arms to pick her up, and Leah held her breath, hoping that Casey would allow him to hold her. Her wish came true.

He pressed a kiss on her cheek and, smiling like a man who'd finally found his way home, headed for the door. "Come on, Mommy. We have to go now."

Casey looked back over his shoulder. "Come on, Mommy."

Leah smiled, but that smile quickly faded as she saw the look in Jan's eyes again. *Yes, it's a farce,* Leah's eyes seemed to say. *But it's for Casey. And it's worth it.*

THE MELANCHOLY of that afternoon turned to stark fear as the sun fell and the kidnappers still had not been caught. More reporters circled her house and hounded her phone line. Her father's calls came every hour. And the police and detectives were no closer to finding the two men who had taken her baby than they had been the day before.

It was only then, as she watched Jeff barbecue hamburgers on the grill on her deck, that she realized how afraid she was. Jeff hadn't made any mention of where he was going to sleep tonight. Surely she couldn't expect him to stay here. For all she knew, he had other commitments, other obligations, possibly other attachments. She hadn't even asked him if he was involved with someone. What if he was in love and wanted to be with her tonight, instead of baby-sitting Casey and Leah?

The phone rang again, and Jeff, who had been balancing Casey on one hip while he turned the burgers, looked up at her. "Don't answer it. In fact, go unplug the phone."

Leah shook her head. "I can't. It could be news about the kidnappers. I'll let the machine get it again."

They listened, and heard the voice of her father, telling her once again that he wanted her to bring Casey and stay at his house that night.

She sighed. "He may be right, you know. One or two nights wouldn't hurt, and we'd be safe."

Jeff flashed her a look and, closing the grill, set Casey down. Taking a step toward her, he assessed her with eyes that she feared could see right through her. And she wasn't ready for him to see all that was there.

"I'm staying with you tonight," he said. "I told you I'd stay until they were caught."

Leah handed him the plate she had brought out. He took it, but she didn't let it go. "I know what you said, Jeff, but why should I expect you to put your life on hold for us? If I went over there, you could go home...."

"But you don't want to go over there," he said. "At least, that's the message you've been giving me."

"No," she whispered. "I don't want to. But I'm getting nervous, Jeff. They haven't been caught yet. I thought they'd be in jail by now. They could come back."

"All right," Jeff said, accepting her fears as valid. "Tell me one thing. Why didn't you want to go to your father's before? Why were you so dead set against it? So much, in fact, that you opted to stay here with me?"

She couldn't tell him the real reason. At least not all of it, for she couldn't handle his scoffing at the feelings he would never believe. "Because I was afraid that if he got me home, it might be harder and harder to leave."

"It's comfortable there, no doubt about it. You'd have everything you need, everything you want...."

"That's not what I mean," she said. "You don't know him. If he got us there, he'd find more and more ways of keeping us there. It was hard to break free, Jeff, but I did it. I don't want to go back."

A knock sounded on the door, and Leah closed her eyes. "Another reporter. I can't take this anymore." Her hands trembled as she pushed them through the roots of her hair, and Jeff put the plate down and set his hands on her shoulders, gently urging her face up with his thumbs.

"You don't have to take it." She met his eyes, her heart beginning to burn at the touch that was so gentle that she wondered if he was even aware of it. "We'll go to my house. Chances are they'll leave us alone there, and if not, well, we won't be quite as bothered by all of it there. My house is a little bigger than this, and the land is fenced, so they can't come up and pound on the door anytime they want."

"Are...are you sure? I mean...I wouldn't be stepping on anyone's toes?"

The moment she asked, she felt silly, for it was blatantly obvious that she was fishing for information on his love life.

"You mean...like a woman?"

She felt her face reddening. "Is there one?"

He let her go and turned back to the grill. As he opened it, a white cloud of smoke billowed out. "Not at the moment."

She felt a smile breaking out over her heart, but she kept it from reaching her face. "Then...I guess it would be all right.

"But Casey..." She looked at the little girl who was chasing a lizard across the deck. "I wanted her to be able to sleep in her own bed."

"Then we'll stay here," he said, turning back to her. "It's your choice. But whatever you decide, I'm not leaving you."

The reassuring way he said that made her heart melt in gratitude...and much more. But along with those feelings came regret greater than any she had ever known. For the reassurances were meant for Casey, not her.

"Good," she whispered. "I mean...I don't want to go to my father's. It helps to know you're here."

Their eyes held for a moment, and finally, he turned back to the grill. "It's ready," he said. "We can eat now."

AN HOUR LATER, as they were clearing the dishes from the table on the deck, a camera flashed. Instantly, they both turned around and saw a reporter standing on the sand below them. "Miss Borgadeux?" he called. "May I have a few minutes of your time?"

Her face reddened, and she grabbed Casey and pulled her back against her. "Go away or I'll have you arrested for trespassing!"

Flashing one more picture before Jeff started toward him, the reporter trotted back around the house.

"*Damn* it," Leah said. "He could have been the kidnapper. How do I know who's a reporter and who's a criminal?"

Jeff took her arm and turned her around. "Hey, take it easy. He's gone."

Tears burst into her eyes like a tropical wave held off by a crumbling sea wall. "When can we leave?" she asked.

He pushed her hair back and cupped her neck. "Right now."

"Great," she said quietly as she grabbed Casey and started inside. "Let's hurry before I lose my mind."

LEAH'S MIND was still intact by the time they got to Jeff's house, set on a three-acre lot surrounded by a chain-link fence in which two Irish setters romped. Outdoor floodlights illuminated the gravel driveway in the opaque darkness. As they pulled in, the dogs jumped up to the van windows, eagerly whining for their owner to acknowledge their itching ears and wet noses.

"When did you buy this?" Leah asked as they drew closer to the house hidden behind an enormous oak tree.

"About two years ago," he said.

That his purchase had happened just a few months after their breakup was obvious. "It's beautiful, Jeff. But it's just you. Why would you buy all this just for yourself?"

"Wanted some permanency," he said. "I got tired of waiting for something to happen." He parked the car and got out to greet the yelping dogs as Casey squirmed in her seat and squealed, "Puppies!"

"They're a little bigger than puppies," he said, reaching into the back seat and unbuckling Casey from her car seat.

Leah tried to focus on the dogs and Casey's reaction, but Jeff's words still hung on the air. "Something like what? What were you waiting to happen?"

He set the suitcase down and looked up at her as if she were an unwelcome intruder on a joyous moment. "I don't know. Look, the house isn't all that big. It only has three bedrooms."

"But you only need one."

"Not anymore, I don't."

He lifted Casey up to his shoulders, and the little girl, who had grown used to him throughout the day, squealed and wrapped her arms around his neck, giggling at the dogs still wagging their tails and nuzzling his legs. His attitude, concerned and caring just an hour before, grew guarded and distant from Leah as he unlocked the house and switched on the light inside.

The living room looked like a decorator's showcase. From the deep velvet sofa to the pecan coffee table and the wallpaper and trims that made the place at once lovely and unlivable, there were expensive and elaborate accessories generously placed throughout the house. None of them seemed to possess anything of Jeff's personality or preferences. It was as though he'd had nothing at all to do with arranging his home.

"Did a professional decorator do all this?" she asked, looking around.

"Most of it," he said.

She touched a lamp that she knew had cost hundreds of dollars. "Jeff, it's beautiful, but... when I knew you before, you weren't the extravagant type."

"Yeah, well, we all make mistakes," he said, taking Casey off his shoulders. "I guess I was trying to prove something."

"Prove what?"

"I don't know! That I wasn't just some slouch who wasn't good enough for the almighty Borgadeux."

"But who were you trying to prove it to?" she asked softly.

"Myself," he said. "That's all."

Casey ran across the room, exploring some of the expensive breakables he had sitting out. Jeff's eyes followed her with adoration rather than worry about his possessions.

"You never had to prove that to me, Jeff," she whispered. "I liked you the way you were."

"You *left* me the way I was."

As if he couldn't sit still under her scrutiny, he got up and set an expensive vase on the mantel, out of Casey's reach. But Leah wanted to continue the conversation. She couldn't leave it hanging.

"Jeff, I can see that you've been successful. But if you don't mind my pointing this out, that only proves my point. If we had stayed together, you wouldn't have had the means to buy any of this stuff. My father would have seen to it."

"But it wasn't the *stuff* I wanted in the first place, Leah," he said with an insufferable weariness that seemed to doubt she could ever understand.

"And it wasn't what I wanted, either," she whispered.

Casey found a tall bar stool, and whined to be put up on it. Jeff obliged.

"You can go check out the bedrooms if you want," he said, changing the subject. "I figure you can stay in the middle one, since it has access to the master bathroom. The one on the end can be Casey's."

She reached down to pick up the suitcase, and Jeff went on. "I plan to have it decorated for her as soon as I can. I want her to spend a lot of time here."

Leah turned back. "What do you mean, a lot of time?"

"I mean, I want to see my daughter on a regular basis, Leah. I want her on weekends, and a night or two during the week. I want her on holidays and, when she's in school, summers."

Leah's face paled. "Jeff, she's too young to be bounced around. She's not ready for this."

"You mean, *you're* not ready for it."

She swallowed. "All right. *I'm* not ready for it."

"Leah, you're the one who wrote this script. I suggest you start preparing yourself," he said. "I'll prepare Casey."

A lump of emotion lodged itself in Leah's throat as she started back to the bedrooms.

THAT NIGHT, AS SHE LAY next to Casey, with whom she had decided to share a bed since the child was nervous about the new room, she stroked her daughter's cheek.

"I love you, Mommy," Casey whispered.

Leah's heart melted. "I love you, too."

Casey looked around, her big eyes taking in the new surroundings enshrouded in darkness, except for the Mickey Mouse lamplight in the corner, which Leah had brought from home. "This Daddy's house."

Leah smiled. It was the first time Casey had called him that, and she regretted that he was across the hall, showering in the bathroom, and hadn't heard it.

Casey smiled. "I like Daddy."

"Yeah," Leah whispered. "Daddy's a pretty good guy, huh?"

"Daddy buy me Tootsie Pops."

Leah smiled. "Daddy spoils you rotten."

"I like Daddy," Casey said again.

"So do I," Leah whispered as her smile faded. "So do I." She stroked her daughter's hair back from her face and whispered for her to close her eyes. In moments, she thought, sleep would pull Casey under its spell. But as tired as Leah was, she knew that sleep wasn't ready for her yet.

She heard Jeff moving around his bedroom, and knew he was out of the shower. Would he go straight to bed or would he stay up awhile?

She shivered as she thought of his words earlier, when he'd told her he wanted Casey on weekends. The thought of handing her over to anyone, even Jeff, chilled her. Reaching down, she grabbed the blanket beneath Casey's feet and pulled it up to tuck around her daughter's shoulders.

Casey didn't stir, and she knew she had found sleep.

Getting up, she slipped on her robe, tied it at the waist and went back into the living room. Except for one small lamp, he had left it dark.

She went to the telephone and decided to call and listen to her messages, in hopes that there would be word on the kidnappers by now. She dialed the number and listened.

Most of the calls from the press had been hang-ups, thankfully, so the rest were primarily from her father. Sighing, she hung up the phone.

"Anything important?"

Jeff's question made her jump, and she turned around. He was leaning against the doorway, wearing only his jeans, which were noticeably unbuttoned at the waist. His hair was still wet and a shadowy stubble darkened his jaw.

"No, nothing. Just some more reporters and my father."

He lingered there a moment, taking in the sight of her white silken robe, and her hair falling straight and silky around her face. "You want some tea?" he asked, finally. "I have decaf."

The fact that he remembered how she loved to drink tea before bed moved her, and she nodded. "I'll get it, though."

She went into the kitchen and he came in behind her, handing her the cups and sugar. He was too close, and his scent was no longer that from *her* shower, *her* soap, but from his. A flood of memories washed over her, and she kept her eyes down, away from him.

"So Casey's asleep?"

"Mmm-hmm." She filled the kettle with water, turned on the burner. She felt her lips quivering at the corners, and she prayed she wouldn't cry. She could go numb for just awhile, she told herself. She could hold back the pain until later. Summoning all her strength, she finally had to look up at him.

He was leaning next to her against the counter, watching her with eyes that held traces of regrets of his own, and a wealth of memories.

Their eyes met, locked, held, and she asked herself where she could hope for this to lead. She was feeding her grief, adding to her remorse, by even entertaining the idea that he could still be attracted to her.

"She called you Daddy tonight," she whispered.

His face changed. "Really?"

"Yes. Just before she went to sleep. She told me she liked you."

His smile was undeniably sexy, and unaccountably vulnerable. "She said that? Really? What were her exact words?"

"I believe they were, 'I like Daddy.'"

He raked his hand through his hair and looked longingly back toward the bedroom where the child slept. "Damn. Why couldn't I have heard that?"

"You will," she said.

He was quiet for a long moment, and his eyes settled on her again. "Thank you," he said.

"For what?"

"For telling me. I know you weren't thrilled with what I said earlier. About taking Casey on weekends. You could have kept this to yourself."

The teakettle began to whistle, and Leah turned around and moved it from the burner. Again, she felt the ache of tears behind her eyes. "I knew you would want to know."

"I did. It helped."

She poured the tea, keeping her eyes averted, but she couldn't hold back the tears pushing into them. He saw them glistening in the soft light, and touched her chin to bring her face up to his. "What's the matter?" he asked. "What are these tears for?"

She swallowed back the emotion in her throat and took a deep breath. "Why do you want to take her from me?" she asked, her voice breaking. "Can't you see that she's all I've got?"

He took her shoulders and turned her to face him. "Leah, I'm not the bad guy. I'm not going to take her from you. I'm her father. I have a right to spend time with her, too, and it can't always be with you there. It's not fair to you or me.''

"But it's not fair to either of us for you to take her alone. You've seen how she clings to me! She's never been away from me one night in her whole life. Even the night she was kidnapped, she still slept in her own bed, with me right there beside her. You may be her father, Jeff, but you're not the one she depends on!''

Her tears fell over her lashes, tumbled down her cheeks, but still he held her shoulders and stared down at her. "She'll come to depend on me over time. I've only had one day.''

Leah covered her mouth to hide its trembling. "Jeff, she's my baby.''

"She's my baby, too,'' he whispered.

"But you have others in your life,'' she said. "You have Jan, and your parents are great. You have two dogs out in the yard, and friends, and probably even a couple of girlfriends. Don't you understand that I don't have any of that? All I have is Casey!''

"If that's the case, it's because you won't let anyone else in your life, Leah. That's not my fault.''

Leah's crying came harder now, and her shoulders shook beneath his hands. She dropped her face into her hand, and tried to hide the tears that had come so easily lately. "I know it's my fault, Jeff. But that doesn't make it easier.''

He watched her cry, and something inside him stirred to life. Some protective instinct—the same one that had assaulted him yesterday when he'd thought Leah was the one who'd been kidnapped—emerged full force. He slid his hands down the silk of her robe and pulled her against him.

She curled into his bare chest, her cheek pressed against his heart, and she felt his hand combing through her hair. "Shh," he whispered. "I'm not going to take her away from you. We can love her together."

She looked up at him, still enclosed in his arms, and raised her hands to his bare shoulders. "Really, Jeff?" she asked on a sob. "Really?"

He wiped her cheek with the pad of his thumb, and cursed himself for allowing those tears to weaken his resolve. "Yeah."

What was he saying? some voice inside asked him. That he would let her have her way? That he would forego a relationship with his daughter just to keep from making Leah cry? Or that he would go on as they had the last day, hanging around in her life, being a third wheel in a family that wasn't really his?

It didn't matter, because for now, the only answers his heart could focus on, were the blueness of her eyes and the redness of lips wet with tears. She kept looking up at him, kept waiting for more promises, but he found he had none to offer her.

She wet her lips, and he saw the way her eyes fell to his mouth. She could feel his heart beating against her hand, he thought, could feel his reaction to her. It gave her power, and he didn't like it. But it was power nonetheless. And he wasn't strong enough to fight it.

Gently cupping her chin, he tilted her face up to his and descended slowly to her mouth. She tasted salty, like warm tears. Her mouth opened to him, as if it came naturally, and his tongue swirled gently against hers.

Her hands slid up his chest, around his neck, and he felt her raise up to her toes. His hands slid down her back, to the hips that fit his palms, and he pulled her against him.

He knew she could feel his arousal, and he could feel hers in the free, complete way she devoted herself to his kiss. He wondered what she wore beneath the robe, if it would slip easily off her shoulders, if she would balk if he scooped her up and carried her to his bed.

He felt her whimper within the kiss, felt her hand slide down his back, felt her pulling his hips closer against hers. She had always been a great lover... the best lover. She had always known what he liked, how he wanted to be touched.

His hand slid up to the neck of her robe, and he slipped one side off her shoulder. A spaghetti strap held her gown, and breaking the kiss, he nuzzled her neck, then slicked his tongue across her bare shoulder, pulling the strap down as he did.

His blood was hot as he felt her hands moving between them, to the open button at the waist of his jeans. Her hand splayed over his flat abdomen, slid lower, lower.

An urgency, a desperation, a hunger that lacked rationale or reason burned like a torch inside him, and he realized that he *had* lost all power. That she, once again, was completely in control of him.

The thought exhilarated, stimulated, excited him.

It also scared the hell out of him.

Pulling out every shred of control he still possessed, he stopped her hand.

Leah looked up at him, her eyes smoky with longing.

"We can't do this," he whispered. "We can't."

That disarming sadness returned to her eyes. "Why not?"

"Because," he said more firmly, "we can't go back. What's done is done."

She slipped her hand out of his, let it drop to her side, and stepping back, adjusted her robe. "You're right," she whispered.

He could see the embarrassment on her face, the humiliation, and he hated himself for putting it there. He had started it after all. *He* had kissed *her*.

And she had responded in a way that would keep him awake all night, keep his heart thudding whenever she came near, keep his hormones pumping for a long time to come. It made him furious.

"Sex was never our problem," he whispered.

She shook her head.

"It was always good," he went on, condemning himself further with every word. "That's why we can't. It would cloud too many things."

She tried to blink back the tears crowding her eyes, but he saw them. "Funny," she said. "I thought it might clear some things up."

"Like what?" he asked. "Like whether or not I'm still attracted to you? Well, you have your answer. I am. Physically, my body reacts just as strongly to you as yours reacts to me."

She didn't let the confession lift her hopes, for she heard the unspoken "but" hanging on the end. "And emotionally?"

"Emotionally, Leah, I'd like nothing better than to never see you again."

She stared up at him, her eyes as hurt as his and tried to breathe. But her lungs seemed to have collapsed.

"But since Casey's involved, I have no choice."

"*We* have no choice," Leah said, lifting her chin. "So I suggest that if you want us both to remember the way you feel, that we keep our distance, both emotionally and physically. That means no more long, wet, scathing kisses."

The subtle reminder that *he* had kissed *her* hit its mark. "Agreed," he said.

"Good." She turned around, starting back to the bedroom, and Jeff stopped her.

"Leah, there's one other thing."

She turned to face him and crossed her arms like a sentinel guarding a fragile treasure.

"This weekend I want to take Casey to meet my parents. Of course, you'll have to come along, too."

Leah's tough facade fell again, and for a moment he thought her tears would return. "Fine," she said. "I guess they deserve that."

"She's their granddaughter," he reminded her.

"I know that," she said. "We'll be ready whenever you say."

He watched her leave the room, then wilted back against the counter. His pulse was still pounding, and his hormones were still whirling. His body was still painfully aware of just how much he had wanted her.

And so was she.

It was a power he couldn't let her have over him again. It was too heady, too seductive.

And when it ended, the power could devastate him. He had let her do it to him once.

She would never have that chance again.

Chapter Eight

Instead of going in to work the next morning, Jeff decided to leave Leah and Casey in his home, where still no one had found them, and visit Borgadeux's detectives personally. The case was going nowhere, and even his own detective was drawing a blank. He wanted to make sure everything possible was being done to catch the kidnappers.

The office of Palm Investigations was smaller and more run-down than he would have expected for one of Borgadeux's teams, and from the temporary sign on the door, it looked as if they hadn't been around for very long.

He went in, saw a few desks scattered around the room, and only two people working telephones and computers, though none was active at the moment. The sight of inactivity gave him a sinking feeling, for it was apparent that the office wasn't all abuzz with worry over the kidnappers.

One of the women looked up when he came in. "Can I help you?"

He shrugged. "Yeah. I was looking for Ben or Willy. My name is Jeff Hampton."

Without getting up or picking up the phone, the woman let out a yell that shook the peeling walls. "Ben, someone's here for you!"

"Comin'!" came the reply from one of the offices.

In seconds, Ben was at the door to his office, and he peered out and seemed surprised to see Jeff. "'Ow ya doin', mate? Didn't think I'd see you again."

Confused, Jeff shook his hand and followed him into the dirty office filled with boxes and new furniture. "Are you moving out of here or something?"

"No, movin' in." He knocked a stack of books off of a chair and gestured for Jeff to take it. "So what brings you 'ere?"

"What brings me here?" The question was ludicrous, and Jeff remained standing and gaped at the detective as he dropped into his seat behind his desk. "The kidnapping investigation, what else? I wanted to see what's being done to find my daughter's kidnappers."

"Well, nothin'."

Jeff wasn't sure he'd heard correctly. "Nothing?"

Ben frowned and leaned forward, setting his elbows on the desk.

"No. Mr. Borgadeux fired us right after the girl was found."

"He fired you! Why?"

"Got me. I thought it odd, too, but 'e paid us more money than we usually make on a case like that, then sent us on our way." He leaned up to his desk, set his hands on it. "I was a mite disappointed, too, if you don't mind my sayin' so. We'd kind of 'oped 'e'd give us more work. We sure coulda used it."

Jeff lowered to the chair behind him, his amazed expression reflecting the profoundness of his rising anger. "Do you mean to tell me that you've never worked for him before?"

"Never," the man said. "Why 'e decided to 'ire us, I don't know. 'E retains one of our biggest competitors in the city. But who am I to argue, right? I thought maybe 'e was lookin' to replace 'em."

Jeff stood up again, and prowled around Ben's office, trying to sort out what he'd just learned. "His granddaughter had been kidnapped. Why would he hire someone he'd never worked with before, when he had an office full of crackerjack detectives already on his payroll?"

"Got me. And why'd he want to call off the 'unt just like that... Well, all I can figure is 'e decided to go back to 'is own PI's after all. Guess we won't get more business from 'im, but at least we made enough to 'elp pay for these offices. Nice, ain't they?"

Jeff looked absently around. "Yeah. Nice." Still battling the questions raging in his mind, he started back to the door. "Well, thank you for your time."

"Right." Ben said, hopping up and holding out his hand. "And just for the record, I apologize for the way we 'auled you outa your office the other day. You 'ave to understand, mate. In a kidnapping where the parents don't live together, one of the first suspects 'as to be the father. Borgadeux almost 'ad a 'eart attack when we started asking questions about you. 'E told us we might 'ave screwed up everythin'."

"Screwed up everything? Why?"

"Guess 'e wanted you to stay in the dark about the kid. But it was Leah who told us to find you. No 'ard feelings, 'ey?"

"None," Jeff said. "Thanks for the information."

He went back to his car and started home, struggling to make sense of what he'd just learned. But there was none to be made of it. He only hoped that this niggling fear in his heart was unfounded.

"I WASN'T HIDING from you, Dad." Leah leaned over to hand Casey the apple she had cut up for her, and cradled the phone with her shoulder. She had returned his call after getting a dozen from him on her machine. The last few had been desperate, furious, and he'd threatened to put out a search on her if she didn't call him to let him know where she was. "I just had to get away from the phone calls and the reporters."

"How was I supposed to know you hadn't been kidnapped, too?" he bellowed. "How was I supposed to know that some sick maniac hadn't found a way into your house...."

"Dad, I'm fine. I'm at Jeff's. It's safe here, and no one knows we're here."

"Safe?" he scoffed. "Is he there with you?"

"No, not right now, but—"

"Does he have guards posted outside?"

"No, Dad, but—"

"Does he have a security system? Do you have a gun?"

She grabbed the phone and switched it to her other ear. "No. He has two dogs, though, and a fence around the property, and the phone doesn't ring off the hook and reporters aren't clustered outside waiting for a glimpse of Casey."

"Well, then you aren't safe, Leah. And this ridiculous stand you're taking in refusing to come home with me is only endangering your daughter's life."

Unable to argue with that, Leah took the cordless phone and crossed the room to sit next to Casey, as if her nearness could hold any harm at bay. Idly, she stroked the child's hair as she spoke. "Have they gotten any closer to finding the kidnappers, Dad?"

"They found a witness," he said. "Someone who saw a man with a little girl who looked like Casey. He was in a green car, and she seemed upset. Ben got a description of the man, and he's working on it."

"Really?" she asked, standing back up. "Can he do something with that?"

"It's a start," he said. "I'm paying them a lot of money to work around the clock on this, darling."

"The man. Was it the same one who took Casey from Anna's house?"

"Could be. The point is, they're making progress. We're going to crack this soon, Leah. But those men are still out there. They got two million dollars from us. They might try it again. The only way you can both be completely protected is if you're here with me."

Leah looked at Casey again and wondered if her father was right. Was she being stubborn? Was she risking Casey's life? She started to say something but heard Jeff's car coming up the gravel drive. "Dad, Jeff's home now. I'll call you later."

"Leah, you can't go on as if everything is business as usual! Give me his address, and I'll come over there and get you myself."

"No, Dad. I won't go with you. I said I'll call you later."

She hung up the phone just as Jeff came in. He was wearing a white dress shirt with the sleeves rolled up, and a pair of jeans. His eyes—as they swept down her freshly washed hair, to the tight tank top she wore, to the short white tennis shorts, to her bare legs and feet—were fatigued and troubled.

Casey smiled and started shyly toward him, instantly making him smile, as well. "Hi, there," he said, lifting her up and dropping a kiss on her cheek. He glanced across the room to Leah. "Who were you talking to?"

"My father," she said. "He threatened to put an APB on me if I didn't tell him where I was, so I called. But there's good news. He said that Ben had found a witness. Someone who saw Casey in the car with a man. He's working on some more leads, and—"

"Ben? He said that? That Ben found a witness?"

Leah faltered. "Well . . . yes. Why?"

He stared at her for a moment, trying to decide whether to tell her that for some reason he couldn't fathom, her father had lied to her. That no one was really working on the case. But he decided now wasn't the time. Not until he had a little more information.

"I guess...I'm just glad to hear they're making some progress."

The awkward, tense silence fell between them again, and Casey held an apple slice up to his lips. "I got apple. Want some?"

Jeff's grin was troubled as he took a bite. "Good," he said. "Thank you."

Trying to cross the bridge that loomed precariously between them, Leah got Casey's napkin and wiped her face. "Why are you back so soon? I thought you were going in to the office."

He shrugged. "I planned to, but I got kind of sidetracked. And I didn't feel good about leaving you two alone."

She let her gaze drop to the floor. "Well, you didn't have to come home. Casey's almost ready for a nap."

"You should take one, too," he said. "You look tired."

"So do you," she whispered.

"Maybe I will. But I have a few phone calls to make first."

The dismal feeling that she was intruding on his life washed over her, and she nodded. "All right. I'll lie down with Casey so you can be alone."

Jeff watched Leah leave the room with Casey, and for a moment after she was gone, he stared at the place where she had stood moments before. Something about the way she had believed her father tore at his gut, and he wondered what the man was up to.

Quickly, he picked up the phone and dialed the number of his own investigator. Almost immediately, the receptionist put him through.

"Yeah, Phil. This is Jeff Hampton."

"I was just working on your case, Jeff."

"Find out anything?"

"No. This case is incredibly clean. You got anything?"

"Maybe." He glanced in the direction of the bedrooms again, and lowered his voice. "I stopped by Borgadeux's detectives today. The ones who were there the night of the kidnapping. They told me he fired them from the case. And now I come home, and Leah tells me that her father told her that these same guys are making a lot of progress. What do you make of that?"

The detective was silent for a moment. "I don't know, but I'm gonna find out."

"Yeah, you do that."

When he had hung up, he sat down and stared back in the direction of the bedrooms. She was in there, lying with his daughter—her daughter. *Their* daughter.

The phone rang and absently, he picked it up.

"Hello?"

"Hampton, put my daughter on."

Jeff bristled at the overbearing tone. "She's sleeping, Borgy, but I'll tell her you called."

"Wake her up. This is important."

He thought of calling him on firing the detectives, but something told him not to. Not yet. The man would only rally with excuses, and cover his tracks before Jeff could get to the heart of it. Still, he couldn't squelch his sarcasm. "Is it about another lead on the case?"

Borgadeux hesitated. "I said I want to talk to my daughter."

"And I said she's asleep."

He could almost see the man's face turning crimson. "I'm warning you, Hampton. If you come between my little girl and me again—"

"Little girl? Are we talking about Leah? She's a grown woman, Borgy."

"She's like a little girl when it comes to making decisions," he said. "She doesn't know what she wants. She needs someone to take care of her."

"I'm doing just fine," Jeff said.

Another moment of silence followed.

"Hampton, before this thing is over, she's going to be begging me to come home, and you're going to be left with your heart splattered like the last time. She was raised too well to ever be committed to a nothing like you. Mark my word—"

Jeff slammed down the phone. "Bastard," he whispered through his teeth.

He got up and went into the hallway, looked through the open door and saw Leah lying on the bed with Casey cuddled up next to her. They were both still, and he wondered if she had fallen asleep as quickly as the child had.

The anger in his heart died by degrees, and he stepped closer, leaning against the doorway.

Lying there like that, so soft and vulnerable, she looked innocent. Not like the selfish heartbreaker Borgy had made her out to be. She looked fragile, and it made him want to protect her.

Crossing the room, he stepped closer to the bed and gazed down at her. What would she think, if he told her that her father had lied about the case? Would she think the best, or would she jump to the silly, ridiculous conclusion that his own imagination was jumping to?

But of course, none of that made sense. Her father couldn't be deliberately obstructing justice by calling off the dogs, could he? He would want to see the kidnappers caught as much as Jeff did. Wouldn't he? Even though their methods were different, their goals were the same.

Weren't they?

The doubts that nagged at him told him not to say anything to her until he had more facts. He had no doubt that Phil would have something for him soon.

Leah stirred, and her eyes fluttered open. She looked up at him with sleepy eyes and frowned.

"What?" she whispered.

Embarrassed that he had been caught watching her sleep, Jeff shrugged. "What do you mean, what?"

"Why were you standing there?" she asked softly.

He turned around, hiding the emotion on his face and started back to the door. "I . . . Your father just called. We sort of got into it again and . . . I thought I might have wakened you."

She sat up, self-consciously pushing back her hair. Checking Casey, she covered her with the afghan at the foot of the bed, then motioned for them to go out.

When they were in the living room, Leah turned around, "What did my father say to you?"

"The usual." He started into the kitchen, and she followed.

"I'm sorry. He never gives up."

Jeff opened the refrigerator, peered inside. "He wants you to call him back."

"Not now," she said with a laugh. "It'll just be another lecture designed to make me come running home."

She noticed that Jeff was staring at the contents, not seeing anything that was there. "What is it, Jeff? What's wrong?"

"I was just thinking. Wondering what kind of man your father is. What he's capable of."

He closed the refrigerator door and leaned against it, studying her with serious eyes.

Not certain what he was after, Leah shrugged. "He means well, Jeff. I'm sure of that. It's just that he's used to being in control. He can't stand the idea that I have a mind of my own."

"No," Jeff said, shaking his head. "I mean…what might he *do?* Before, when you talked about why you left me, you said he was going to ruin me. What kind of thing did he tell you he'd do?"

Leah sighed and left the kitchen, went back into the living room and sat down at the hearth, where the fire was crackling. Jeff followed her.

"Leah, answer me. I have to know."

"He said that he had contacts with your financiers. That they would pull the money out from under you. He also said there were rumors he would circulate about your business. Rumors that would ruin you professionally."

"Pretty tough words for someone who means well."

"Yeah, well…" She stopped, wet her lips, and went on. "You would have lost it all if we had stayed together."

"I'm a carpenter," he said. "I work with my hands. Nobody can ever take that away from me."

"You underestimate my father," she whispered.

He looked at her for a long moment, thought of how he had blamed her those two years, how he still blamed her, for screwing up his life. Did she really think she had *saved* it?

Memories of the kiss that night, the way her body had fit so familiarly against his, the way she had tasted, smelled… assaulted him with heart-rending force. That he could let her get to him that way infuriated him.

Hauling his thoughts back in, he stood up. "I have to go," he said.

"Go? Go where?"

Anywhere, he wanted to shout. *Anywhere but here where I have so little control.*

"To the office," he said. "I'll probably be back before Casey wakes up."

She watched him brood on his way to the table where he kept his keys, and giving her one last look over his shoulder, he left the house.

FOR OVER AN HOUR after he left, Leah sat alone in the growing dusk of his living room, arms hugging her knees, and tried to find the source of the gnawing pain in her soul. She was getting nowhere with him, because he would never forgive her for doing what she had to do. For being who she was.

She leaned her head back on the chair and tried to think of ways to make him stop hating her so. It was a feeling, an awareness, that she was not able to stand.

Because in her heart, she still loved him.

She closed her eyes and imagined a scenario in which she confessed to him, and he took her into his arms and told her that was what he wanted and needed to hear, and made slow, heartaching love with her until the sun came up.

But people didn't really live happily ever after, did they?

She got up, went into the kitchen and found a frozen roast in the freezer, some potatoes under the sink and various other things that had the makings for a good pot roast. Trying to get her mind off her heartache, she began to prepare him dinner.

When the roast was in the pressure cooker and there was nothing to do but wait, she went to the ironing board she had seen set up in his laundry room and turned on the iron. He ironed his clothes each morning before he dressed, she had noted, probably because he didn't have the time to iron them all at once, and he wasn't self-indulgent enough to send them out to be done.

She went into his bedroom, found all his wrinkled shirts and three pairs of jeans that had been left in the dryer until the wrinkles had set in and took them back into the laundry room.

Casey woke up an hour later, and as if sensing that it was safe to come home, Jeff came in soon after. Immediately he smelled the roast.

"What's that?"

She smiled. "Pot roast. I hope you weren't saving it for anything special."

He shrugged. "No. You cooked it?"

"Yes, I cooked it."

"I didn't know you could cook."

"There's a lot you don't know about me," she said.

She went back into the laundry room, where she had just finished ironing before Casey had gotten up, and brought out his clothes on hangers.

"What's that?" he asked again.

"Your clothes," she said. "I ironed them so you wouldn't have to."

He set Casey down, stared at her with confusion. "Why?"

"You seem to have a lot to do," she said. "It was something I could do to show my appreciation. Besides, I was bored."

"You could have watched television or taken a walk...."

"I wanted to iron your shirts," she said.

Before that baffled look had the power to sink her heart again, Leah went back into his bedroom to hang up the shirts.

THE SCENT OF ROAST wafted over the house, and suddenly Jeff was assaulted with the feeling of home... a feeling he hadn't ever felt in this house. There was dinner cooking on the stove, an adoring child at his feet, a woman in his bedroom, familiarly hanging his shirts back in his closet. The intimacy of what she had done, of going through his things and finding needs that she could fulfill struck him all at once. It made him want her more. But that desire made him desperately need to hang on to the anger he'd worn like a shield for so long.

They ate as if they were a real family, both telling Casey to sit up, to eat her carrots, to chew before swallowing. They passed the butter and the salt and talked about their daughter. It was nice. But it was also deceiving.

That night, as Jeff was putting Casey to bed, she looked up at him and framed his face with her little hands. "I like you."

His heart plunged then leapt, and he sat down and settled his soft, misty eyes on her. "I like you, too, Casey."

He pressed another kiss on her puckered mouth, gave her a tight hug, then backed away from the bed.

He caught the scent of Leah before he saw her, and he turned around. She was standing in the doorway in a long white robe, and her hair, just washed, was shiny and full around her shoulders. She was smiling, and he knew that she had heard the exchange between father and daughter. It didn't threaten her that her daughter could love someone else, he realized. It actually made her happy.

He diverted his eyes and slipped past her. Their arms brushed, and his heart jolted, but still he did not meet her eyes. "Good night," he whispered.

"Night," she said.

He left them alone in the room, and rather than staying up watching television as he usually did, he decided to take a shower. A cold, icy shower. A shower that could wash those irrational feelings away and make him forget how one look from Leah could make his heartbeat accelerate. A shower that cleaned his body but did nothing to cleanse his mind.

CASEY WAS ASLEEP in moments, but Leah found that sleep eluded her. It was around the corner, just out of her grasp. Just like Jeff.

She loved him. The admission seemed to make her feelings easier to deal with. She had established the problem, the source for her misery. Now all she had to do was act on it.

She had heard him take a shower, and the scent of his soap and steam still wafted across the air from the open bathroom. She wondered if he'd gone to bed. She wondered if he, too, were awake. She wondered if he was thinking of her.

Fleeting memories of an afghan tucked around her, of waking up to see him watching her, of the kiss that had seared both their souls and startled him into a retreat, assaulted her. He did want her. She knew that. But it was her job to make him *want* to want her.

And the first step would be telling him how she felt.

Slowly she drew out of bed, ignored her robe, wearing only the long silky negligee. Not knowing what she hoped to accomplish, if anything, she took a deep breath. Quietly she padded down the hall carpet and stopped at the open doorway to his bedroom.

He lay there motionless, staring at the ceiling, and for a moment, she didn't know if he saw her. Without a word, she started toward him.

He looked at her then, confused alarm flashing across his eyes as she drew nearer, and she saw his eyes dash down to her breasts, thinly covered by the white silk. His eyes moved back up to her face, anticipating what was to come. She saw desire there, lust and some emotion she couldn't name.

She also saw him tensing, as if he were the hunter's prey being stunned with a bright light.

She sat down on the edge of the bed, set her hand on his bare chest and stroked upward to his stubbled chin. Her eyes were serious, apprehensive, as she gazed down at him.

"Jeff, there's something I have to tell you."

She saw him swallow. "What?"

Her finger traced the curve of his ear, then slipped through the soft hair just above it. Slowly she bent down to kiss him.

His mouth opened in response, and their tongues grazed in a reluctant mating dance that neither seemed powerful enough to fend off. She felt his heart pounding beneath her hand, felt his breath seeping out in relief, felt his arms moving up her bare arms. One thumb moved across the silk at her nipple, inciting it to bud and peak in response.

He pulled her farther down, and more boldly now, his hand moved over her breast, palmed it, stroked it. His other hand moved down her partially bare back, to the hips covered with lacy panties.

Joy and ecstasy danced in her soul as she realized that he wasn't going to send her away...that he was going to love her as she needed to be loved...that he was going to allow her to love him as he needed to be loved.

Slowly he pulled her toward the center of the bed, laid her down and rolled onto his side. He slipped his knees between her thighs, and his hands began to move more urgently over her. His tongue played heart games in her mouth, and his ragged breath was swallowed up by her kiss.

His hands moved over her face, her shoulder. He slid her strap down, and the silky fabric slipped down over her breast.

His movements became more urgent, more rapid, as his desire grew. He broke the kiss, dipped his head down and grabbed her nipple in his mouth. She whimpered beneath his ministrations, and that very whimper seemed to heighten the urgency more.

He moved above her, and she could feel his tumescence beneath the briefs he wore. Then suddenly he peeled her panties off her and discarded them along with his own. She caught her breath as he filled her, and began to move harder, faster, with a contagious delirium that drew her to the brink of madness.

His body shuddered with the quick release, his heart pounding in dangerous rhythm, his skin perspiring and sliding against her.

Exhausted, he untangled himself from her and fell onto his back. She lay there beside him for a long moment, feeling the sudden rush of coldness—of incompletion. Lifting herself up on an elbow, she slid her hand across his abdomen and kissed the corner of his mouth.

His eyes came open, and she could see the smoky confusion coloring them. "Why did you do that?" he whispered. "I have to know why."

"Because," she whispered, her words a breath across his lips. "I love you. I've always loved you. I've never stopped loving you."

Roughly, he framed her face in his, stared at her with stricken eyes, as if he, too, had a confession to make. But after a second, she saw the shutters swinging shut over his eyes.

He pushed her away.

Tears burst into her eyes. "Jeff, I—"

"Don't," he said. "Don't say that to me again. I don't want to hear it."

"But it's true."

"It's not true," he argued. "It can't be true. Not after all this time. Not after all you've done."

Trying not to let the tears explode in front of him, she slipped out of bed, straightened her gown and found her panties lying on the floor. Grabbing them, she left the room without looking back.

Chapter Nine

The car radio droned out Tina Turner's cynicism as she wondered "What's Love Got to Do with It," and for the first time, Leah knew the meaning of the song. Love had nothing to do with it. Absolutely nothing. The lovemaking they had shared the night before was separate and apart from any connected emotion. Jeff had stroked her, cherished her, held her, quivered within her.... But it was only for a moment. And the moment passed.

They had gotten ready for the trip to see Jeff's parents without speaking to each other. Their avoidance of each other's eyes took a herculean effort, but Leah managed it. Anger, planted the night before, now grew and blossomed in her heart. But it was her problem to deal with, and she vowed to grit her teeth and endure the day for Casey's sake. If she found Jeff's distance disheartening now—and she did—she realized it was nothing compared to what she expected from his parents.

She had met his parents once before, when she and Jeff were in love and she'd believed nothing would ever separate them. But that was before her father had found out about him. Then, Al and Florence Hampton had embraced her as part of the family. Warmth and inclusion came easily for the couple who had spent twenty years operating the Hampton House, a country-music bar that was the hot spot of Brooksville's baby-boomer crowd. Everyone who came into their bar was family to them, but those who came into their home were treated even more warmly.

She wondered how that would change now.

Jeff had called yesterday and told them he was coming, that he was bringing a surprise and that they would like it. Jan, who'd claimed she didn't want to miss the looks on their faces, and added that Jeff might need a buffer to keep them calm, had gone on up the night before.

Leah didn't kid herself into denying that she was nervous. She was sick-nervous. The kind of nervous that clamped a vise over her chest and kept her from being able to breathe. The kind of nervous that made all the other negatives in life look even worse. The kind where tears seemed just behind her eyes, waiting for the worst possible moment to ambush her.

She thought about how stupid it had been to make love to Jeff last night. She thought how cruel it had been of him to accept it, then turn her away. She thought how miserable the day would be, considering that his parents would no doubt hate her for keeping Casey from him all this time.

The silence was so thick between them that she wanted to scream, or reach out and shake him, but it finally occurred to her that, if he did open up and start to talk, she really had nothing more to say. There came a time when words didn't matter, and actions mattered even less.

But still there was that little girl sucking her thumb in the back seat, the little girl who was getting attached to her daddy, the little girl who was now a part of both their lives. It was the hell Leah had to pay for keeping her secret.

As HE DROVE, Jeff thought of the way Leah's skin had felt beneath his hand, the way she had tasted, the way they had fitted together like they had never been apart.

And he thought of her proclamation of love. The one he had ridiculed. The one that had sent her away in tears.

He was a bastard, he thought. He had hurt her deliberately, and he didn't even know why.

Quickly reeling those traitorous thoughts back in, he told himself that he did know why. It was because he still didn't trust her, and he hated himself for giving her power over him again. When she had loved him, then articulated that love, he had lost a little more of himself to her.

"I need to go potty," Casey said from the back seat.

Jeff glanced in the rearview mirror. "Potty?" He looked at Leah. "I thought she wore diapers. I thought that potty-training stuff was something she was just starting."

"Well, maybe she's more ready than I thought."

She looked in the back seat and smiled at the child. "We'll find you a potty, sweetie. Won't we, Daddy?"

Jeff glanced over his shoulder. "Sure will. Right up here's a McDonald's. If you go in the potty, I'll buy you an ice-cream cone. How about that?"

Casey smiled around her thumb and told him it was just fine.

Off guard, Jeff met Leah's eyes, and they shared a smile. It was one of those rare, unexpected moments of intimacy—spoken without a word—that the common love of Casey evoked. He knew there would be many more of those, and he supposed they'd be just as hard to distance himself from as their lovemaking last night.

TWO EMPTY POTTIES, a wet diaper and a melted ice-cream cone later, they pulled onto the street in Brooksville where Jeff had grown up. The house was set about a hundred yards from a big pond that contained a score of catfish that his father raised, and sat snugly in the shade of three giant oaks. Leah knew Casey would love it here.

Jeff parked the car on the gravel drive, and that vise over Leah's lungs tightened. She was here for Casey, she told herself again, and however his parents wanted to treat her, that was fine.

Jeff looked over at her. "You ready?"

She tried to hold back those threatening tears. "Not really."

"It'll be okay," he said. He twisted in his seat and looked at Casey. "How 'bout you, Casey? Are you ready to meet Grandma and Grandpa?"

Not taking her thumb out of her mouth, Casey nodded. Slipping out of her seat, Leah went back to

Casey and grabbed a wipe from her diaper bag. From her peripheral vision, she saw his parents and Jan come out of the house. Quickly she wiped the ice-cream cone off of Casey's face and hands, and removed her bib.

"Where we going?" Casey asked, looking past her to the people approaching the car.

The words got caught in Leah's throat as she unhooked Casey from her car seat and set her down on the floor of the vehicle.

"Mommy staying?"

This time Leah made herself answer. "Yes, darling. Mommy's staying with you."

Jeff opened the door, smiling like a proud father with a day-old infant. "Come here, short stuff," he said.

Casey took one look at the people approaching her and backed into Leah's arms.

"It's okay," Leah whispered, holding Casey and stepping out. "I'll hold her."

Coming closer, Florence Hampton looked at Leah, then at Casey, then at Jeff, the wrinkled lines in her forehead defining her puzzlement at Jeff's "surprise." "Hello," she said finally, and Leah didn't miss the coolness in her voice. "Jeff didn't tell us you were coming."

"I said I had a surprise, Mom," Jeff said, dropping a kiss on her cheek.

His mother tried to laugh but fell short. "I thought you'd gotten a new car or a haircut or something...."

"It's better, Mom," he said, setting a possessive hand on Casey's head. "Mom, Dad, this is Casey. She's your granddaughter."

"Our *what!*" The words of both parents came simultaneously, and Jan covered her mouth and began to laugh.

"I love it," she said. "I should have had the camera ready."

Her mother turned on her, as if she'd been somehow responsible for the shocking news. "Did you know about this and not tell us?"

"Just a couple of days, Mom," Jan said. "Jeff swore me to secrecy."

"Why?" Florence turned back to her son. "This child is at least . . . how old *is* she?"

"Two," Leah said quietly.

"For two years you've had a beautiful little daughter, Jeff, and you've kept it from us? *Why?*"

"I didn't know until a couple of days ago myself," he said.

Florence Hampton's face blanched and she turned her condemning glare back to Leah.

"It's a long story, Mom," Jeff said. "Come on. We'll go inside and I'll tell you everything."

His mother hesitated, and Leah saw the fine mist forming in her eyes as the woman looked at the child in Leah's arms. Her hand trembled as she brought it up to touch Casey's curls. "May I . . . hold her?" the woman asked.

For a second, Leah thought Casey would go to her, and she allowed herself to fantasize about sitting in the car all day—out of the chill of his family's hatred of her—while they got to know Casey inside.

But Casey recoiled from Florence and threw her arms around Leah's neck.

Her fantasy quickly vaporized, and kissing Casey's head and holding her securely, Leah started toward the house. "I'm not leaving you, sweetheart. I'm staying right here."

Casey's death grip embrace didn't loosen as they went into the house.

"SO WHAT ARE YOUR PLANS?" Al Hampton, Jeff's father, asked the question of both Jeff and Leah as Florence read Casey a book on the floor near Leah's feet.

"Plans?" Jeff asked. "We have no plans. I'm staying with Leah and Casey until the kidnappers are caught, and then there will be visitation—"

"No marriage?" Al cut in. "No resumed romantic affair?"

Jeff met Leah's eyes, and she knew he was thinking of last night. She looked away.

"Mr. Hampton," Leah said, "I didn't' tell Jeff about Casey so I could somehow trap him into a relationship. I was wrong to keep Casey from him—"

"Damn right you were wrong."

She faltered, took a deep breath and started again. "I realize that. And now I'm willing to make it up by letting him play a part in her life. That's all. I'm not out to rope a husband."

"It's complicated, trying to raise a child in two separate households. A child is not a possession to be passed around."

Leah's heart sank at the reality of his words, and her sad gaze drifted to Casey, who was warming up to her grandmother. It wouldn't take that long for her to trust Jeff and Jan and their parents as much as she trusted her. Before she knew it, she'd be *asking* to come see them. Still, the memory of Jeff's words the other night, when he'd promised not to take Casey from her—how much had been in reaction to her tears, and how much would he honor?

"We aren't going to do anything to hurt Casey," Jeff said. "Leah's a good mother. And I can be a good father."

"She needs good *parents,*" his father said. "She needs a family. Not a fragmented facsimile of one!"

"This is the way it is, Dad," Jeff said on a sigh. "We only have this to work with."

Jan, also on the floor with her mother and Casey, piped in. "Come on, Dad. What do you want him to do? Marry her?"

The word was thrown out with such contempt that Leah's lips tightened, and she glanced toward the floor, wishing desperately for a means of escape.

"Hell, no, I don't want him *marrying* her," Al threw back. "I just want him to realize that this isn't going to be a picnic."

"I realize that, Dad. Leah and I will work it out somehow. Trust us."

Jeff's eyes met Leah's again, and she looked at him with a profound sadness that stirred his heart. His eyes, too, saddened. Getting up, he took Casey from the floor, kissed her cheek and held her close to him. "The bottom line, Dad, is that I have a little daughter. And nothing anyone says or does is going to change that. She's mine. And she's yours, too, if you want her."

Casey sneezed twice, and instantly the room exploded into a flurry of activity. Florence jumped up and grabbed a tissue from a nearby box. Al rose and began a baby-talk chant of "God bless you, God bless you." Jan's laughter overrode it all, as if the sneeze had been one for *America's Funniest Home Videos*.

And Leah stood back, feeling less a part of her daughter's life than she'd ever felt in her life.

AT MIDAFTERNOON, THEY SAT down to eat the traditional feast that Florence Hampton usually reserved for Sundays, but had broken the rules and cooked today, instead.

Casey could want for nothing, for Jan and Florence fussed over her with each bite she took. Jeff and his father sat at opposite ends of the table, talking over the noise as if they hadn't seen each other in years.

In the midst of all the hubbub, Leah was the outcast. The one whose eyes no one would meet. The one no one addressed. The one who could have fallen through a hole in the earth, and no one would have cared.

After a while, when Casey was occupied with chocolate pudding, Leah left the table quietly and went outside. Sitting down on the steps, she dropped her face into her hands and let the tears that she had held back all day fall at last.

The door opened behind her, and someone came out. She looked up and saw Jan.

"Tough day, huh?" Jeff's sister said without much sympathy.

Leah nodded.

"You know, we haven't meant to be rude to you, Leah. I can see that you feel as awkward as we do."

"You haven't been rude," Leah lied. "Everything's fine. I didn't expect to be welcomed here with open arms."

Jan sighed and sat down next to her. "Look, I know it's hard on you, but you have to understand. When you left Jeff... well, he hurt pretty bad. He didn't recover for about a year. He brooded and was irritable all the time. No one could talk to him. And he went on these wild spending binges, like he had to prove to the world that he would have been good enough for the Borgadeux. It was hard on the whole family to see him that way."

Leah smeared a tear across her face. "I know that. I don't blame them for hating me. And I don't blame him—"

The door opened, and Jeff stepped out, looked from Jan to Leah. His eyes lingered on Leah's tears, and quickly, he dashed accusing eyes to his sister. "Leave her alone, Jan. She hasn't done anything to you."

Jan came to her feet. "For your information, I didn't do anything to her, either. We were just talking."

"Leave her alone," he said again.

Leah looked up, surprised at his defense of her. "Jeff, she wasn't—"

"That's okay," Jan bit out. "I'm going in."

The door closed behind her, and Leah met his eyes, forgetting to hide her tears. He was no stranger to them these days. "You didn't have to do that, you know. I can take care of myself."

He lowered himself to the step beside her, and with both palms she wiped the remnants of tears from her face. "Where's Casey?"

"My mother took her to the back to see the kittens. Any minute now she'll be screaming for you."

Leah started to get up. "I'll go ahead and see about her."

"Wait." He caught her arm and pulled her back down. "Wait."

She looked at him, bracing herself for the pain that came so abundantly whenever he was near.

"I wanted to tell you that . . . I'm sorry for the way they're treating you. It's hard on them."

"That's exactly what Jan was saying," she told him. "But I don't have to be told. I can see how hard it is."

"But it doesn't make it easier for you, does it?"

She shook her head, and looked out over the trees across the road. "The last time I was here, they welcomed me like I was one of them. And I *felt* like I could be. Like this could be my family. I've never had that before, you know. Not really. That's something that I still don't think you understand."

"You had your father," he said, that cool edge returning to his voice.

"My father is a controller, Jeff," she said. "He tries to love, but he isn't good at it. It's unnatural for him, somehow. But for your family, it's so easy. They took Casey in like they had known her since birth, and I just can't help wishing—"

"That they could take you in, too?"

It seemed so ludicrous that she couldn't make herself say it. "I can't help wishing that things could have been different."

"So do I," he whispered.

They sat next to each other for a long moment, staring off into space, seeing the same dream. But the dream was only that, and they both knew the impossibility of it ever being fulfilled. Too much damage had been done. After a moment, Leah stood up. "I'm going to check on Casey."

He came to his feet and started to follow her around the house. "Leah, before you go, I have to ask you something. My parents wanted us to come to their bar tonight. They want to show Casey off. I thought we could stay for a couple of hours, then drive home late. Is that okay?"

She shrugged. "Sure, whatever you say."

Then not looking back at him, she left him standing there and went to find her daughter.

LEAH SURMISED from the difference in his parents' moods that he had had a word with them. She was back inside, rocking Casey as she drifted into a nap, when Florence came in and gave her a cool smile.

"It must have been awful for you when she was kidnapped."

Leah nodded. "It was."

"Are you afraid? Of them coming back again, I mean?"

Leah looked at the woman who had such warm lines around her face. This coldness she displayed toward Leah was accomplished only with great effort, she told herself. It didn't come naturally to the woman. "Yes, I'm afraid. But I'm grateful to Jeff for helping us through this."

The woman compressed her lips and nodded. "You know, it was quite a surprise to hear about Casey."

"I know," she whispered. "I'm really sorry for that."

Florence nodded again. "I hope you'll keep your word and let Jeff see her after all this is over. I hope you'll let him bring her back here. A lot. Already we've gotten attached to her."

She closed her eyes and tightened her embrace on the sleeping child. "I promise," she whispered.

Florence left them alone in the shadows of the living room, and unable to put Casey down, for it had been a cold morning with only the child who cared about her, Leah continued to rock her throughout her nap.

JEFF STOPPED at the doorway and looked in. He saw Leah rocking the sleeping girl in her arms. Her own eyes were closed, and her head was leaned back.

It was the most beautiful sight he had ever seen. His child, and the woman he—

He stopped midthought and hauled his emotions back. The woman he once loved. The woman with whom he had conceived a child.

He wasn't sure how long he stood there, just staring at them, but his mother noticed it. When he finally turned around to go back into the kitchen, Florence was shaking her head.

"You're still in love with her, aren't you?"

"What? No, of course not. Not after what she did to me." He went to a pan of brownies and mashed some crumbs with his finger.

"Unfortunately, Jeff, your brain doesn't always dictate what's in your heart. I saw the way you looked at her."

"I was looking at Casey, Mom. I love Casey."

"And earlier today, when she left the table and you turned on us for being so cold to her, were you thinking of Casey then, too?"

He shoved away the brownies and looked at his mother. "Yes, as a matter of fact. Leah's my daughter's mother. We have to get along. You have to get used to the fact that she's a permanent fixture in Casey's life."

"Which makes her a permanent fixture in yours."

He set his hands on his hips and cocked his head impatiently. "What are you saying, Mom?"

"I'm saying, son, that sometimes convenience can make us believe what we want to believe. Knowing how complicated it is to raise a child separately, you might convince yourself that she's changed, that you're still in love with her, that you can be happy with her."

"Mom, you don't have to worry."

"I can't help worrying," she said. "I don't want to see you hurt again."

"Leah's not going to hurt me again," he said, feeling the heat rush to his cheeks. "She brought me to my knees once, but I'm stronger for it now. I'm not going to let it happen again."

BUT THAT NIGHT, at the Hampton House, where Jeff and Jan had spent most weekend nights throughout their lives, Jeff wondered if he could really stand behind those words.

Leah sat at the corner of the table with Casey tucked in her lap, swaying to the live music of the country band. A dim red light cast a glow over her head, painted the tops of her cheekbones, her nose, her lips....

He drew his eyes away and looked out over the dance floor, where lovers danced and laughed and flirted. His eyes gravitated back to Leah and Casey, and he saw the delight on his daughter's face at the excitement generated by the live music and dancing. Slowly standing, not knowing just whom he was approaching—Leah or Casey—he went around the table.

Casey smiled up at him, making his choice easy.

"Casey, will you dance with me?"

Casey cast her big eyes out over the dance floor and nodded.

He reached down, picked her up and held her against him with one arm extended as they went to the dance floor.

LEAH WATCHED JEFF dancing with her daughter, swinging the little girl around, dipping her and making her laugh louder than she'd ever heard. A soft smile played on her lips, and she decided that that sight was even more beautiful than the sight of Casey alone.

She saw him look back at her, saw him grinning with amusement at the way Casey was trying to throw herself into the dips and keeping her own kind of rhythm to the song the band was playing.

"He's good with her," Jan said, popping a peanut into her mouth.

Leah nodded.

"He's going to be a good father."

"He already is," Leah said.

The song ended, and Jeff started dancing Casey back to the table as friends applauded. Leah stood up to reach for her, but Jan came between them.

"Did you dance with Daddy?" Jan asked Casey. "Did you like that?"

Jeff surrendered the girl to his sister as the band launched into another tune, and his eyes met Leah's. She started to sit back down, but he stopped her. "You want to show Casey how it's really done?" he asked with a smile.

"Me?"

His grin disarmed her completely. "Yes, you. If I recall, you and I cut a pretty good rug together."

We did a lot of things well together, she thought. *But none of it meant anything.* Swallowing, she glanced back at Casey, saw that the child was preoccupied with Jan. "I don't know, Jeff."

Not taking her reluctance for an answer, he took her hand and pulled her to her feet.

The song the band decided to play at that moment was anything but a "cut the rug" song. Instead, it was a slow, weepy love song that forced couples to come together, to embrace, to sway against each other's bodies.

She hesitated. "We...we could wait for the next song."

He pulled her against him and took her hand. "There's nothing wrong with this one."

Their faces were so close that she could feel his breath on her lips. The way he held her brought back images of last night—images she desperately wanted to escape. "I just didn't think you'd want to...."

"Neither did I," he said. "But life's full of surprises."

She was silent for a moment, trying to decipher his words. Was he making some kind of revelation or just making conversation? For the life of her, she didn't know. They danced quietly for a long while as she tried to steady her runaway heartbeat and the fragile hope she knew better than to entertain. His face moved close to her ear, and she could feel the warmth of his breath. "You've been great today, Leah," he whispered. "I really appreciate it."

She dropped her forehead against his shoulder and refrained from telling him that she really had no choice. That it had been pure hell.

"And last night..."

Her head snapped up, and she met his eyes. He hadn't mentioned their lovemaking since it had happened. His eyes were smoky and direct as they looked into hers.

"Last night was wonderful...even better than I remembered."

She kept her eyes fixed on his, stricken, waiting for whatever was to come next.

"I'm sorry for what I said afterward. I can be a real SOB sometimes."

"You weren't being an SOB," she whispered. "You were being honest. You were saying what you feel. I can't blame you for that."

She saw the turmoil on his face as he looked down at her, and she wondered if it was her imagination that he had tightened his hold on her infinitesimally. Was he beginning to despise her a little less? Was he beginning to like her again?

She knew that love was too much to hope for, so she didn't even allow herself to. But maybe he didn't want to push her away anymore.

The song ended, but he didn't let her go as the dancers around them broke up and applauded. It was seconds later before he released her, and even then his eyes held hers with an intensity she wanted desperately to understand.

Finally he turned away from her and started back to the table, where Casey had just noticed that Leah was gone and was reaching for her.

Leah took her and, holding her close, glanced at Jeff over her head. He was watching her.

A tiny thrill ebbed inside her as she sat back down. Something was on his mind. Something to do with her alone—apart from Casey. Anticipation swirled in her head and her heart, and she couldn't wait to get back home with him.

Chapter Ten

The ride home was quiet, tense and rife with anticipation. The animosity had disappeared, and in its place was a disturbing feeling of confusing desire. Jeff feared saying anything, so he said nothing.

They reached his house, and while Leah put the sleeping child to bed, he hung back in the living room, deciding he needed to keep his distance until his feelings were more in his control. He couldn't feel desire for her. Sleeping with her again would be cruel. It would be dangerous.

It would be wonderful.

Trying to shake the thoughts from his mind, he went to his phone and checked the messages on his machine. One was from his detective, and said to call him tonight no matter how late he got home.

Quickly, Jeff dialed the number. The phone was answered on the first ring.

"Phil? It's Jeff. What have you got?"

"You're not going to believe this," the detective said. "Are you sitting down?"

Jeff switched the phone to his other ear and grabbed a pencil. "Let me have it."

"I did some checking on Borgadeux today. And I found out that the morning after the kidnapping, he deposited two million dollars back in the same bank account from which he had withdrawn it the day before. I don't know about you, but I smell something rotten."

Jeff frowned, unable to make sense of it. "You mean he took it out the day of the kidnapping, we gave it to the kidnappers and then the next morning he re-deposited it?"

"Looks that way to me."

"Maybe he liquidated something to make up for it. Maybe he transferred some funds to cover it, or sold some stock...."

"I checked. The money seems to have come from nowhere, except out of that same account the day before."

"I don't get it." Jeff glanced toward the bedrooms, then lowered his voice. "What do you think is going on, Phil? Any ideas?"

"I don't know," Phil said. "Unless maybe the man was involved, which makes absolutely no sense. Why would he want to stage his granddaughter's kidnapping?"

"To manipulate his daughter, maybe?" Jeff asked, not realizing he had mumbled his thoughts aloud.

"Maybe. You'd know better than me. I've got a few more things to check tomorrow. Be available in case I find something, all right?"

"Yeah, sure."

Leah came into the room just as Jeff was hanging up. Her hair was disheveled from the day and the drive, and her eyes were sleepy and more aware than he wanted to admit. What little makeup she had worn today had all but worn off. Still, she looked beautiful. Too beautiful to walk away from.

"Any news?" she asked.

For a moment, he thought of telling her what he had learned, but it seemed premature. It could be a coincidence, he thought. And there was no use speculating about it until he knew more.

"None," he said. He leaned back against the couch and slid his hands into his pockets and looked at her standing before him.

"Well…it's late," she said. "I guess I'll go get some sleep."

"Yeah." He looked down at his feet, then stood upright, facing her. "Leah, I really appreciate your cooperation today. I know it wasn't easy."

She swallowed. "It could have been worse."

He looked down at her lips, pink and soft and wet, then moved his gaze back to those eyes, watching him, reading him. He wondered if she saw everything.

"Well . . . good night," she whispered.

"Wait."

His eyes dropped back to her lips, and his face moved closer. She didn't turn away, didn't back down, as he came as close as he could without touching her. He told himself to stop it now, that there was too much at stake, that if he let this happen again, there would be no more controlling his feelings.

"I want to kiss you," he said.

She felt his breath on her lips, and wet them again. "That's not a good idea," she whispered without moving away.

"No," he said. "It isn't, is it?"

They looked at each other for a fragment of eternity, hearts pounding so loudly and so hard that they weren't sure whose they heard.

He lowered his face, and she swallowed. His lips grazed hers, jolting her heart, and before taking her completely, he whispered, "But I'm gonna do it anyway."

When he took full possession of her lips, there was no turning back. It was as if they had signed in blood, sold their souls and now were sucked into the black spell that would own them forever.

The kiss grew deeper, and he pulled her against him, his hands moving over her in memory of last night's loving. She responded as he knew she would, as she always had, and that response filled a need deep within his soul, a need that it had always filled, a need that had always lain empty when she was not there.

He kissed her temple, her forehead, the bridge of her nose. Her trembling subsided as he kissed the corner of her mouth, then the center of her bottom lip, wet and smooth and downturned.

His mouth met hers, opening a floodgate of feeling, of latent passion, of burning desire that he didn't know he had endured for so long.

His kiss was like a drug that dulled her pain and replaced it with a burning of her own. She slid her arms up to his shoulders, laced her fingers through his hair.

Without realizing what he was doing, he slipped his arm beneath her legs, lifted her, and not breaking the kiss, carried her to his bed.

Jeff told himself that when he loved her this time, there would be no regrets, no recriminations. He would deal with the consequences of his feeling. He would live with it and whatever it meant.

They made love, discovering, once again, that the bond destiny had forged between them years before was still not broken.

AFTERWARD, AS SHE LAY soft and sleeping in his arms, he buried his face in her hair and tried to sort out all the misery in his life. He hadn't felt this whole, despite all the anger and confusion, since the day she had walked out on him.

But the pain wouldn't go away. It was like an old friend, a convenience, something he clutched to his heart like a shield. He couldn't forget what she had done to him by walking away and keeping Casey a secret.

But that anger wasn't as sharp as it was before, for now it came with a stream of reasons behind it. Reasons she had given him, reasons that only now possessed some validity. Borgy was a mean-spirited bastard. And if he was capable of lying and conniving to manipulate his daughter, maybe he would have tried to ruin Jeff's life.

He would have failed, Jeff thought, but how could Leah have known that? Deep in her heart, he knew that she knew that her father could be a heartless monster, that he could be capable of kidnapping.

Deep in her heart, perhaps, she had believed that Jeff would be ruined if she didn't do as her father told her.

Still, it was so hard to forgive her.

She stirred in his arms, and he held her tighter, not willing to let her go. Her hair smelled of lemons, and it felt like satin against his stubble. His heart felt heavy, not with the weight of her head, but with the weight of his emotion for her. He did love her, but that frightened the hell out of him.

"Oh, Leah," he whispered, knowing she didn't hear. "Make me believe in you again. Make it so I'm not afraid to love you again."

He looked down at her face, so soft and shadowed as she slept, and he knew that it was a wish that would die without reaching her heart. He doubted she could have made it come true, anyway.

THEY SLEPT TOGETHER, wrapped in each other's arms, until Casey woke them the next morning. As if nothing unusual lay in the fact that she'd found her parents sleeping together, the child climbed into bed between them and demanded the Gummi Bears cartoon.

They ate breakfast together, passing meaningful smiles and sensuous glances across the table, though neither of them spoke of what the night had meant. Neither chose to spoil the pure and unhampered feelings of the day with talk and speculation.

When the dishes were done and he had showered and dressed, Jeff called the office and learned that there was a problem on his work site. "I have to go to the site for a couple of hours," he said, "but I don't want to leave you. Do you and Casey want to come with me?''

"No," she said. "I have to make some phone calls. I want to make arrangements to have someone open my shop for me tomorrow. We'll be all right alone while you're gone."

He left them, Casey playing in his living room and Leah straightening the kitchen, and smiled all his way to work.

IT WASN'T LONG AFTER Jeff had left that Leah got Casey busy molding clay, and decided to check her machine for her messages.

Her father's voice, demanding and angry, came across the line three times. But the fourth call was from another voice... a voice she recognized... the voice that sent a shiver up her spine and made her heart plunge.

"Casey will never be safe," the voice said. "We could take her from her bed, or from your car, or from your patio. You could even find her washed up on that beach you live on. If I were you, I'd keep a little extra cash handy. You never know when you might need it again!"

"Oh, God!" She dropped the phone and jumped back, as if it had burned her.

"What, Mommy?"

She put her hand over her mouth and backed farther from the phone. "Oh, my God! Oh no!" Quickly reigning her thoughts in, she turned and grabbed Casey up off the floor. "Come here, baby. Let Mommy hold you."

Seeing her mother's state, Casey didn't argue.

Trembling, Leah ran back to the phone, snatched it up and began dialing the number of Jeff's work site that he'd left near the phone. It rang four, five, six, seven times before she realized that no one was in the office.

"Damn," she whispered, hanging it up.

It rang beneath her hand before she'd even let it go, and she brought it to her ear. "Hello?"

"Damn it, girl," her father shouted. "Where the hell were you last night? I've been trying to call—"

"Daddy!" She tried to steady her voice, but a sob escaped her. "They called back, Dad. They said—"

"Who called? The kidnappers?"

"Yes! Dad, Jeff's not here and I'm scared!"

"I'm coming over," he said. "I'll be there in fifteen minutes."

"No!" She swallowed and tried to stop her whirling thoughts. "I need to talk to Jeff first. I can't just pick up and go with you."

"Damn it, Leah, stop thinking of yourself and think of your daughter for a change! Her life is in danger! Do you want to take a chance with those lunatics?"

Casey put her arms around Leah's neck and hugged her, and Leah sobbed again. "You're right, I know. Oh, God, you're right."

"They can't get to either of you at my house," her father said. "It's the only right thing to do, Leah. I'll be right over."

"All right." The words, once out, seemed to fill her with relief to counter the fear in her heart. "All right, Dad. I'll be ready."

She hung up the phone and stared at it, wondering if she'd done the right thing. Her father had won, but if she didn't go with him, they could all lose. And it wasn't a gamble she was willing to make.

Setting Casey down, she took her hand. "Come on, pumpkin," she said, wiping her tears. "We have to go pack."

"Where we going?" Casey asked.

"To visit Grandpa for a while," she said.

"Daddy coming?"

Tears burst to Leah's eyes again, but fear propelled her onward. "No, honey. Not yet. But we'll see him later, okay?"

She tried to call Jeff again before she left, but there was still no answer in the trailer on his work site. Instead, she left him a brief note, telling him about the phone call, and letting him know how she could be reached. He would be furious, she knew, but there wasn't time to go into a lengthy explanation. There would be plenty of time for that later.

IT HAD TAKEN HOURS but Jeff solved the problem at the work site. He'd spent the entire time thinking of getting home and basking in Leah's smile and her sensuality again.

No, their problems hadn't miraculously evaporated. Some of the anger was still there, along with the pain and the knowledge of her deceit. He couldn't forgive that. He couldn't forget. But that desire riding higher in his soul seemed to be more pronounced. Despite himself, he wanted to hold her again. Wanted to taste the honey sweetness of her. Wanted to breathe in her scent.

And when Casey took her nap, he wanted to make love to Leah again, as he had done last night.

What he found, instead, was an empty house and a note that shattered his world. He stared at it for a moment, not believing it, when finally he started through the house, denying it with every step. The rooms were clean, empty, as if they had never been there.

"No!" he shouted, kicking the wall with his foot and leaving a scuffed imprint on the wallpaper. "No, damn you! You can't do this to me again!"

He ran to the phone, dialed Borgy's number, and listened as a servant answered the phone.

"Borgadeux residence."

"I want to speak to Leah!"

"I'm sorry," the maid said. "She isn't taking any calls."

"Damn it, tell her it's Jeff! Put her on the phone right now."

"I'm sorry—"

"No!" he shouted, gripping the phone as if it were the maid's neck. "Damn it, put Borgadeux on the line. Let me speak to him."

He waited a moment, then heard Leah's father's amused voice as he took the phone. "What's the matter, Hampton? You're not still a sore loser, are you?"

"Let me speak to Leah, Borgy!" he shouted. "If you don't, I'll make so much trouble for you you won't know what hit you!"

"Go to hell, Hampton." The phone went dead in Jeff's hand, and he yanked it out of the wall and flung it across the room. It landed with a ringing thud.

Grabbing his keys, he started to the door, deciding to pay a visit to the "Borgadeux residence." If the man wanted to play the game this way, then by God, Jeff would fight back. And he would use every resource available. He wasn't going to let Leah do this to him again.

THE ROOM her father had reserved for Casey was decorated with disturbing detail in Laura Ashley wallpaper with coordinating drapes, bedspread and accessories. Some of the most elaborate toys she had ever seen filled the room next to Casey's, never before touched by a child's hands but waiting for the day Casey would enter the room with delight and wonder.

Leah wanted to keep her from going in there now, but it was impossible. Her father had already dangled the temptation before the child, and Leah was powerless to stop him.

In fact, she was powerless to do much of anything now that she had succumbed to her father and come back into his house. Yes, she was safe. Nothing could break through her father's security.

But nothing could break out, either.

"You two settling in all right?"

She turned around and saw her father standing in the doorway, smiling with peculiar pride at Casey on the floor playing with a dollhouse that was too mature for her. "How could we not?" she asked. "It's been a long time since I've had everything done for me."

"You deserve it," he said. He walked into the playroom and patted Casey's head. "Dinner's at seven. I've been looking so forward to this. The family, all together."

He turned back to Leah, and smiled with a sincerity she had seen very rarely in him. "I've been so lonely without you, Leah. This house gets very cold when its empty."

"I know, Dad," she whispered.

"I want you to make yourself at home," he said. "As if you never left. The servants are all at your disposal. You can do whatever you like."

"Except leave," she said.

He frowned and stepped toward her. "Leah, it's just until the kidnappers are caught. They can't touch you here. You can wipe them out of your mind, forget they ever existed. You can go on with your life and—"

"My life?" she asked, her voice a dull monotone. "What life? I have a business to run, Dad. I can't do that locked away in here. And I have a home. And Jeff—"

"You did just fine without him before all this. You don't need him now."

"But he's Casey's father, Dad. I promised him he could see her. When he calls, I'm going to tell him he can come here whenever he wants. He can see Casey here, and if you try to stop him, I'll have to leave."

"No, I wouldn't do that," Borgadeux said. "Your business can wait and Jeff can wait. What's important is your safety. That's the only thing."

She looked at the phone that had sat so silent all afternoon. The maid had always answered the unit downstairs, then rung whatever room Leah was in if the call was for her. Jeff hadn't called, and she couldn't understand it.

"Are you sure Jeff hasn't called?" she asked. "Are you sure Tessa just didn't forget or something?"

"Sorry, sweetheart. No word."

She sighed. "Then I guess I should try him again. I just don't know where he could be."

"Who knows what the carpenter son of a bartender does with his time?" he asked. "He'll call when he gets around to it."

OUT AT THE FRONT GATE, Jeff's car pulled up to the little security house where two guards stood watch.

A benign-looking guard with a German accent came to his window. "May I help you?"

Jeff got out of the car and faced the guard squarely. "I'm Jeff Hampton, and my daughter is in there. I want to see her now, or I'm—"

The other guard joined the one facing Jeff, and he could see them both bracing themselves for a fight. "I'm sorry, Mr. Hampton, but we have strict orders not to let anyone through those gates."

"Wait a minute! I have the right to see my daughter! Tell Leah I'm here. I want to talk to her."

"She isn't taking calls," the guard said. "Now if you'll just get back in your car—"

"Damn it, she can't do this! She can't run this time! There's a child involved!"

The guards grabbed Jeff by each arm, and he tried to shake them off. Strength honed by hard outdoor labor enabled him to make it difficult for them, but they had him almost in his car when he heard footsteps on the other side of the locked gates. He shook free of the guards and went to the gates, facing Lance Borgadeux with venomous rage.

"You get Leah out here right now, Borgy!"

The guards grabbed Jeff again, and Borgadeux laughed. "That's right. Put him back in his car. If he won't leave, call the police."

Jeff struggled. "I'm warning you. If you try to keep my daughter from me, so help me God, I'll get a lawyer! I'll make you walk through hell with me, Borgy!"

"Notice that I'm growing weak in the knees," Borgadeux said. "My hands are trembling. I might even faint. Now, gentlemen. He's worn out his welcome."

Before Jeff could shout further threats, the guards took him to his car, and one of them drove him, himself, out of the drive.

Leah never even knew he had come.

CASEY WAS SLEEPING later that afternoon, when Leah went downstairs to confront the maid who answered the phone. She didn't like the woman, for she rarely looked her in the eye when she spoke to her, and it gave Leah the uneasy feeling that she wasn't someone she could trust.

"Miss Beel, are you sure that I haven't had any calls today?"

"None, miss."

"But have you answered the phone every time it's rung? I mean, maybe the cook got it or—"

"I always answer the phone, miss, except for your father's private line. No one's phoned for you."

"I see."

Sighing, she went to the phone in her father's study, closed the doors and once again dialed Jeff's number. Again, his machine answered, and again, she left a message. "Jeff, why haven't you called? I need to speak to you. Please, call me at my father's as soon as you get—"

The machine beeped as the phone was snatched up, and Jeff yelled, "Damn it, Leah! Why did you do it?"

"Jeff? Why did I do what?"

"Why did you run away again?" He was out of breath, as though he'd just run into the house.

"I didn't run away. Haven't you gotten any of my messages? Didn't you get my note?"

"I got your note and left," he said. "I haven't been home to get any godforsaken messages. I've been too busy brawling with those guards at your front gate!"

"Here? You were here?"

"Hell, yes, I was there. They wouldn't let me in."

"What?" She turned around, but the maid had left the room. "It must have been a mistake. You should have called first so I could make sure they let you in."

"Damn it, Leah, I've called a dozen times today. That maid of your father's keeps telling me you aren't taking calls! Short of helicoptering in and landing on your roof, there wasn't any way to reach you."

"I can't believe this." She felt her face mottling with patches of heat. "Miss Beel told me no one had called, and I've been calling you all day. Jeff, I told my father when I came here that it was only with the condition that you could come whenever you wanted. I'm not trying to keep Casey from you, but if you read the note you know that the kidnappers called again. I felt like an open target, Jeff, and I couldn't reach you—"

"Leah, your father is conning you. And you're letting him do it."

"Jeff, I had no choice. This is not a question of pride anymore. It's a question of survival. I can't risk Casey's life just to make a point!"

"Leah, she's my daughter, too."

"I know that, Jeff. And I'm not taking her from you. And what had started happening between us...I don't want to destroy that. I just want to be safe until those men are caught."

"Leah, there aren't any *men,* damn it! It's a hoax. It's all a stupid, cruel hoax!"

"What?"

His breathing was still heavy, but he lowered his voice to a calmer pitch. "Leah, listen to me. I didn't want to tell you this before I had more facts, because I don't know what it means. But you have to know before you let your father manipulate you any further."

"Manipulate me? He's trying to *protect* me!"

"Listen to me!" he said, silencing her. "I lied to you about there not being any news. There is some news. A lot of it."

"What? Tell me."

He plowed his hand through his hair and turned around, trying to decide where to start. "A couple of days ago, I went to see Ben and Willy. You remember? The detectives your father hired.''

"And?''

''And they told me that your father fired them from the case the night Casey was found.''

"He what?" She shook her head. ''Well, there must be some explanation.''

"Is there?'' he asked. ''Didn't he tell you just yesterday that Ben was working on some leads?''

She sat down on a Chippendale chair next to the telephone table, suddenly dizzy from the confusion. ''Yes. And even today he mentioned them. Why would he lie, Jeff?''

"I found out that he had never worked with them before, that he had just hired them that day for this. He retains a very good, very reputable detective agency, but he went to these fly-by-night guys to find his granddaughter. Does that make sense to you?''

"No!'' she said, her voice shaking. ''He said he'd worked with them a lot.''

"And when I checked with the other agency he often uses, they hadn't been called in on the case at all.''

She sprang to her feet and began pacing. ''Why? Why would he call off the search?''

"Maybe he didn't want anyone to dig deep enough.''

Her head was beginning to throb. ''That doesn't make sense, Jeff.''

"Right. It doesn't make sense. And neither does the other thing I found out. Your father made a two-million-dollar deposit back into his bank account the day after the kidnapping. And there's no record of any stock or property being liquidated, or any transfer of funds from any other accounts."

For a moment she froze, trying desperately to put the pieces together. "What are you saying?"

"I don't know," he whispered. "You tell me what your father is capable of."

"Not that," she said. "Not having my baby kidnapped for some bizarre manipulative reason. He wouldn't do that, Jeff."

"I know it's hard to believe, Leah. I know—"

"He wouldn't, Jeff! He's my father! He has a lot of problems, a lot of shortcomings, and he'd do a lot of things. But not that!"

"Okay, take it easy." He was quiet for a moment, listening to the breathing pattern of her crying.

"He wouldn't," she said again. "He wouldn't. Jeff, you don't believe that, do you? You don't think—"

"I don't think anything," he whispered. "I don't know anything."

She sucked in a deep, cleansing breath and wiped at her tears. "Well, I do. There are kidnappers, Jeff. They did take my baby. And they'll take her again. My father is the only one who can protect me right now, and if you can't handle that, then I'm truly sorry."

"Leah, I'm not making this up. It's all true."

"I have to go check on Casey," she said. "I'll call you later." And before Jeff could say any more, she had hung up the phone.

Chapter Eleven

Leah stared at the telephone for a moment before she backed away from it. Her lips trembled, and she hugged her arms around herself and started for the door.

Jeff was wrong. There was some explanation for the things he'd said. Her father would never do anything that malicious, that underhanded, simply to manipulate her.

Wiping her tears with a trembling hand, she went back upstairs and into Casey's room. Lance Borgadeux was standing over the bed, smiling down at the napping child.

He loves her, she thought. *He would never do anything to hurt her.*

"She's beautiful," he whispered.

Unable to speak, she tried to smile.

"Just like you when you were a baby," he went on in a gentle voice that belied the ugliness Jeff had accused him of. "You didn't suck your thumb, but you had a pacifier. They told me not to let you have it, that it would ruin your teeth, but I couldn't help it. I let you have it.''

She leaned back against the wall and gazed at her father, loving him despite his tyranny—as she had always loved him.

''Remember that day, when you were almost three, and the dentist handed you the wastebasket and told you to throw the pacifier away? You tossed it right in and never asked for it again.''

''I was afraid of him,'' she said. ''I've always responded to fear.''

''Well,'' he said. ''It was just a pacifier.''

And my baby.

She reeled her thoughts back in and told herself again that none of what Jeff had said was true. Her father was strong, decisive, authoritative...even threatening.

But not malicious.

She cleared her throat and gestured toward the door.

''Dad, I need to talk to you,'' she whispered.

Still smiling, he nodded and came out into the corridor, where a handwoven Aubusson rug ran the length of the floor. Her mother had designed it herself and had laid it the month before Leah was born. She hadn't lived to see her daughter walk on it.

''What is it, sweetheart?''

Leah looked up at him, dread darkening the color of her eyes. ''I just talked to Jeff. He said he's been trying to call, but that Miss Beel wouldn't put the call through to me. He also said he was turned away at the gate. That you knew he was here and didn't tell me.''

"Oh, honey." He sighed and stroked her hair, and gestured for her to sit down on a gold-gilded bench beside the wall. "You were so upset when you came here this morning," he said. "I wanted you to have time to get your bearings before he started badgering you to risk your child's life and go back to him."

Tears sprang to her eyes, and she swallowed. "I'm only staying until the kidnappers are found, Dad. You do realize that, don't you?"

"Of course," he said. "I didn't expect anything else."

She looked down at her hands that were suddenly very cold and folded them to conceal the trembling. "Has . . . has Ben come up with anything else?"

Her father sat down next to her and patted her clasped hands. "A few little morsels of clues here and there, but nothing substantial."

She felt a lump forming in her throat, a lump that made it difficult for her to speak. She knew he was lying, but she couldn't face what that meant. "But he is still looking?"

"Of course," her father said. "Night and day."

Her heart plunged farther. So he was lying about the detectives. That didn't mean he had staged the kidnapping.

"About Jeff . . ." she said, and her voice sounded thin and shredded. "I told Jeff he could come here anytime, Dad. I told him—"

"Leah, wake up," he cut in gently. "That two-bit construction worker is after only one thing. Your money."

Leah moved her gaze back to her father. "I don't have any money, Daddy. You cancelled my trust fund when I moved away from home."

"Well, I plan to reinstate it. Besides, if he isn't after your money, he's after Casey's. He's manipulating you to get control of her trust fund."

"Then cancel it, too. Give the money to charity. Casey doesn't need your money. I can provide for her. As soon as the kidnappers are found I'm going back home—"

"And what if they aren't found?" her father asked, his voice rising by degrees. "What if the detectives and cops can't come up with anything? What if weeks, months go by, and they're still not caught? They could get her again, Leah. This time, they might kill her! Meanwhile, you have to be settled *somewhere*. It's not good for a child to move back and forth—"

"Dad, listen to me—"

"They'll terrorize you for years, kidnapping that child and blackmailing you. They could take her from her bed, or your car, or from your patio—"

As he spoke, she rose to her feet, staring down at him with eyes that, for the first time in a long time, saw him as clearly as Jeff did. "How do you know what they said?"

Her words cut into his monologue, slicing to the heart of his deception.

"What? What who said?"

"What the kidnapper said on the machine? How did you know?"

"You told me."

"I didn't tell you that. And it's kind of strange that you would know it, because those were their exact words."

"Well, that doesn't surprise me." He turned around, but she could see the distress on his face, the same distress that he harbored when he was cornered in a less-than-straight business deal on any given day. "All it takes is a little common sense, a little thought, to figure out what they're capable of."

"I guess they're capable of just about anything," she whispered.

It was at that moment that she realized the things Jeff had said were true—that her father had used her baby, manipulated her, lied, stolen and cheated. It was at that moment that she realized the extent of the prison he had created for her.

Borgadeux hugged her and pressed a kiss on her cheek. "You don't have to be afraid, darling. I'll always be here."

"You're right, Dad," she whispered flatly. "We can always count on you."

THAT EVENING when her father was busy on the telephone in his study and the staff had all retired to their own quarters, Leah sat in the bathroom, watching Casey frolic in her bubble bath. A froth of white smattered across her nose, and she giggled and lay down, stretching out and pretending to swim.

"I'm Little Muh-maid," she told Leah.

Leah smiled. "Wash your face, Little Mermaid."

Casey scooped a handful of bubbles and rubbed them across her face, as if that would do the trick. In-

stead, it made her look like a poor imitation of Santa
Claus. Leah tried to smile again, but her mouth quivered and tears filled her eyes.

What am I going to do?

The question had gnawed at Leah's mind since her
conversation with Jeff, reminding her incessantly that
her father had lied, that Jeff had been right.... But
what did it mean?

She had run the gamut from wanting to confront
her father with the dirty truth to wanting to run as far
and as fast as she could. Confrontation seemed a
waste of time. Borgadeux was a smooth operator. He
could talk his way out of anything, and turn the tables
around as if she'd been the one who'd committed a
crime. If he would have her baby kidnapped, there was
no telling what other horrors he could exact in the
name of love. As long as she was near him, she was at
his mercy. And merely going back to her own little
house and her own little life were not enough. She had
to get farther away. So far that she would never have
to fear his threats again.

The decision jelled in her mind even as she pulled
Casey from the tub and dried her off. They would go
tonight. And by the time her father realized they were
gone, it would be too late to get her back.

But as her resolve hardened, her heart ached, for she
knew that leaving her life behind meant leaving Jeff,
too. He could never understand her need to run, and
their relationship was far too precarious, too embry-
onic, for her to expect him to go with her.

Smearing her tears across her face, Leah dressed
Casey and quickly packed the few things they had

brought here with them. Then, when she was sure that no one was around to stop them, she grabbed the child and left from the back door.

"Where are we going, Mommy?"

"Home," Leah whispered. "Be quiet now. We don't want anyone to hear us."

She spirited the child to the huge garage, where her father kept his limousine and two Jaguars. The key, as always, was in the ignition, for the garage was locked each night. She put Casey in one of the Jaguars, hooked her seat belt, then punched the digital code on the remote control garage opener. The lock disengaged, and the door quietly came up.

The car windows were tinted black and as she pulled to the front gates, the guards assumed she was her father. Without hesitation they opened the gates, and she pulled out onto the street.

A breath of profound relief escaped her as she drove farther from her father's estate. She glanced over at Casey, saw her sucking her thumb and staring up at her with wide eyes. "It's okay, sweetheart. Everything's going to be fine now."

THE DARKNESS HAD INVADED Jeff's house like an army of demons, surrounding and attacking while he sat alone on his recliner, staring at the nothingness Leah had left behind. Between two fingers, he held the neck of a half-empty, lukewarm bottle of beer—the strongest thing he'd been able to find in his house to quell the aching in his soul.

Like the percussive beat of a cavalry's hooves, he heard a knock at the door, then his sister calling, "Jeff? Are you in there?"

He sat still, paralyzed, for he didn't want to confront Jan right now. I-told-you-so's were particularly hard for him to swallow. Especially when his own heart screamed them louder than ever.

He heard her try the knob and vaguely remembered that he'd forgotten to lock it. It came open, and Jan stepped inside. "Jeff?"

"When people don't answer the door it usually means they don't want company."

Jan flicked on a lamp and gaped at her brother, sitting in the shadows. "Jeff, are you all right? You sounded so bad on the phone—"

"I didn't feel like talking. Still don't."

Jan closed the door and crossed the floor. She sat down facing him, not hiding the poignant concern on her features. "Jeff, what's wrong? Is it about Leah?"

"Let it go."

"Jeff, what did she do?"

A slow, heartless, whispered laugh escaped him. "She got me again, Jan. She moved back in with her father. Only this time, I guess I deserved it. I knew better than to let her back under my skin."

"Damn her!" Jan came to her feet and paced across the room, then turned back to him. "I knew she'd do it. I told you—"

"Save it."

She let the thought die and came to her brother, bent over him. Her eyes glistened as she looked into his. "I'm sorry, Jeff. I'm so sorry. But what about Casey?"

"Who knows?" He pulled the recliner's lever and dropped his feet. "She says she isn't cutting me off, but Borgy won't let me near them."

Jan sat on the chair's arm and hugged her brother, but he didn't respond. "You're in love with her again, aren't you?"

Slipping out of her embrace, Jeff stood up and ambled across the floor, rubbing the back of his neck. "Yeah," he whispered. "I guess I am. And that makes me the biggest kind of fool." He turned back to Jan, his eyes reddening. "I thought she had changed, that she had separated from her father. That she wouldn't do this again. But then that bastard told her lies, and she believed every word."

"It's Casey," Jan whispered. "She's scared out of her mind for Casey."

"But it's all a lie, Jan. He set her up. It was a hoax, and I tried to tell her—"

"A hoax?" She frowned and stood up. "Jeff, are you sure?"

"As sure as I can be," he said, his voice rising as the anger took hold of him. "The man will do anything, *anything* to get her under his wing. He's dangerous, Jan. He's ruthless. And now Leah and *my* daughter are his puppets, and I'm locked out."

"Leah doesn't strike me as the kind of woman who could be anyone's puppet, Jeff. Maybe you just need to give her some time."

"Time to do what?" he asked. "Time to make Casey forget she ever *had* a father? Time to let Borgy fill Leah's head with more lies and raise Casey to be just as afraid to move as Leah is?''

The phone rang, and Jeff threw back another mouthful of beer and ignored it.

"Do you want me to get it?" Jan asked.

He shook his head. "I don't want to talk to anybody."

"Maybe it's her, Jeff."

"I especially don't want to talk to her. Damn her, she's ruining me, Jan. She's ripping me up again—"

The phone kept ringing, and his voice trailed off as he looked at it with dull eyes. His face turned red, and finally, he threw down the bottle of beer, watching it shatter on the floor as he snatched up the phone. "Yeah?" he yelled.

"Jeff!" It was Leah's voice, rushed and breathless.

"Leah?"

"Meet me at my house," she blurted. "I'm on my way there now. And hurry."

"Leah, what's wrong? How did you talk your father—"

"You were right about him, Jeff." Her voice wobbled, and he could hear that she was crying. "He lied. He must have set up the whole thing. We'll talk when I see you."

Adrenaline filled his veins, and his heart swelled with relief. Suddenly the anger was gone, and in its place was a different emotion that set him back on track and opened the dark places in his soul again. "I'll be right there," he said.

The phone went dead, and Jeff hung it up and swung around to Jan, who had bent over to clean up

the mess. "I've got to go," he said, life returning to his
eyes. "She needs me."

Jan didn't utter a recriminating word as she watched
her brother bolt out of his house to rescue the woman
he had cursed just moments ago.

JEFF WAS WAITING in her driveway when Leah pulled
up to her house and quickly she threw the car into
Park and pulled Casey out. "Hurry," she told him
when he reached the Jaguar. "I've got to go in and get
some things. He'll realize I'm gone soon and come
after me."

Baffled, Jeff took Casey and the suitcase and followed her in. "Leah, what are you doing?"

She ran to the bedroom and grabbed two more
suitcases, opened them and began emptying the contents of her drawers into them. "Leah! Where are you
going?"

"Away from here," she said. "Anywhere!"

"Wait a minute!" He sat Casey down and went toward her. "Leah, talk to me. Stop just for a minute
and look at me!" When she kept throwing things into
her bags, he took her arms and turned her from the
suitcases. Suddenly she wilted like a flower snapped at
the stem, and he felt the sobs shaking her body.

"He did it!" she cried, muffling her horror with her
hand. "You were right, Jeff. He staged it all. My own
father. How could he have done that to me? To my
baby?"

Jeff gathered her up and held her close, as though
his own warmth could dispel the chill in her soul. Be-

side the door, Casey watched her mother weep. Her thumb went to her mouth.

"It's the betrayal that hurts so much, Jeff. That someone I love could deceive me so deliberately. Could betray me in the worst kind of way...."

"Leah, what are you about to do?" he asked. "What are the suitcases for?"

Leah reined in her shattered emotions and looked up at him with the deepest dread she'd ever faced. "Oh, Jeff," she whispered sadly. She wiped her face with a trembling hand and shoved her hair back as she slipped out of his arms.

"I could prosecute him, but how could we really prove what he did? A bank account, his detectives fired. Those aren't enough. Or we could expose him publicly, but the press would turn it into some sort of greedy tabloid feud, and Casey's life would be marked forever. I don't want her to grow up with that."

Jeff stood motionless, watching her pace the length of the room as she spoke. Casey, looking distraught, herself, went to Leah and held up her arms to be picked up. Leah bent over and lifted her.

"The only way to beat him, Jeff, is to make sure he never sees Casey again," she said, pressing her face against Casey's and closing her eyes. "I'm willing to do whatever that takes. I won't let him do this again."

"Then you aren't going back there at all?"

"No!" she cried. "I want to get away from him. So far that he can never find us."

She turned around to Jeff, the sadness in her eyes so profound that Jeff wondered if anything could ever wipe it away completely. "Jeff, I don't want to take her away from you,'' she whispered, ''and I don't want to leave you, either.''

''I don't want you to.'' He swallowed the intense lump of emotion in his throat and fixed his gaze on the desperation in her eyes.

''I know I have no right to ask this of you, Jeff, but if you wanted to come with us...''

For a moment, he didn't answer, and a barrage of fears assaulted her. She'd had no right to ask. No right to assume that his feelings for her had been reborn. Just because they were lovers again, didn't mean that he loved her. ''I'm sorry,'' she whispered. ''I didn't mean to presume anything about you... about us.... What's happened between us...''

''Presume.''

Her words died out, and she stared at him for a moment. ''What?''

''Go ahead and presume,'' he said. ''You'd be right.''

She caught her breath on a sob and covered her mouth with her hand. ''About what?''

''About the way I feel about you.''

''And... and how is that?'' she whispered. ''Don't make me presume.''

He went to her and Casey, and slid his arms around her. His expression was more serious than she'd ever seen it. ''The other night, when we made love, I realized a lot of things, Leah.''

Her tears clouded her eyes again. ''What things?''

''The way I still feel about you... even apart from Casey.''

She swallowed and clung to every word . . . even the ones he hadn't yet uttered.

"And then . . . when you went back to him, Leah, I didn't think I could take it. Losing Casey again . . . losing you . . ."

"I don't want to leave you," she said, realizing he wasn't going to say the words but accepting what he had said instead. "But I have to go. Please understand."

"Where, Leah? Where are you going? Are you going to just leave your business? Your home?"

"Yes," she said. "And I don't *know* where I'm going. Just . . . anywhere. I can get a job in a town where no one knows what the Borgadeux name means. But I understand if you can't do that with me, Jeff. You'd have to leave everything, too, and if you can't, I really do understand." She sobbed and turned her face away, anticipating his answer.

Jeff rubbed his face, wondering at the irony of her leaving him once before to save his business, and now asking him to leave that same business for her. The greatest irony of all, however, was that it didn't require a second thought.

"Let's get packed," he said simply.

Leah muffled a cry of joy, and he crushed her against him again, holding her with all the grief and despair he had felt for the past two and a half years. No matter what it meant, he wasn't going to let her father take her away from him again. This time, Borgy would be the one to grieve.

LESS THAN A HALF HOUR later, Leah strapped Casey into her car seat in Jeff's car and made one last trip through the house for anything they might have forgotten.

Jeff was waiting beside the passenger car door when she came out of the house. His eyes were sober, yet serene, as he framed her face and stroked her cheekbone with his thumb. "You realize what this means, don't you? We won't come back here. We're saying goodbye to everything."

"I realize it," she whispered. "But are you sure you do?"

"I know what I'm doing," he said.

He kissed her then, long and hard, without the inhibitions he had possessed the first two times they had made love this week. This time, a full heart of emotion, of commitment not yet expressed, of hope too new to look fully upon, played in their kiss.

"Let's go, Daddy," Casey called out.

Jeff broke the kiss and leaned into the back seat, looking at the child who had never called him Daddy before. "What, Casey?" he asked, his voice shredded. "What did you say?"

"Let's go, Daddy. I ready."

He stood, paralyzed, for a moment, savoring the sound of the word he had longed to hear and trying desperately to stop his mouth from trembling and his eyes from welling.

When he looked back at Leah, he saw the tears glistening on her cheeks, and he smiled. "She called me Daddy."

"I know," she whispered. "And the look on your face means more to me than anything I could think of."

He drew in a deep, shaky breath and pressed a kiss on Casey's puckered little mouth. "I love you, Casey."

"I love you, Daddy. Let's go!"

Laughing, Jeff slipped into the driver's seat and closed his door. "Okay, Casey. We're going."

In less than an hour, Casey was sound asleep and quiet had settled over the car. Jeff looked over at Leah.

"Where are we going? Any ideas?"

"I don't care," she said. "Anywhere."

He smiled, but a hint of a shadow darkened his eyes. "I can't believe you're willing to do this."

"I can't believe you are."

"Why wouldn't I?"

She dabbed at the tears in her eyes. "Because of the way you've felt about me for the past two years."

He frowned and stared at the road for a long moment. Streetlights illuminated his face briefly, then cast it in darkness again. "Well, like I told you, maybe that's changing."

Leah leaned across the seat, following her impulse to hug him. He slipped his arm around her, possessively, and she knew that he was healing from the hurts she—and her father—had inflicted upon him. She couldn't expect sudden pronouncements of love, or any emotions articulated. She would take whatever he gave her, whenever he was ready.

Awkward with the newfound tenderness between them, Jeff broke the silence. "We'll drive for a few hours and stop in Fort Walton Beach,'' he said. ''We can get a hotel room, spend the rest of the night there and decide where to go from there.''

She nodded. ''Dad's probably discovered we're gone by now. He's probably going nuts.''

''He won't find us,'' he said. ''We'll be able to relax in Fort Walton. And then we can think.''

IT WAS AFTER MIDNIGHT when they checked into a hotel in Fort Walton Beach, and it was only after Jeff let them into the room that Leah realized he had gotten only one.

He carried the sleeping child in first, laid her in the middle of one of the double beds, and gently covered her with her blanket. He took her Bunny Fu-Fu from Leah and tucked it under her arm.

''You and I can sleep in that one,'' he whispered.

Her eyes collided with his, then quickly skittered away. ''All right. If you'll get the suitcases, I'll stay here with Casey.''

He nodded and went back out to the parking lot. Leah locked the door behind him. Turning back to the beds, she watched Casey sleep. She looked so peaceful, so unhampered by turmoil and deceit, so satisfied.

And that was how Leah felt. It was funny, she thought, but her father's deceit had actually liberated her completely. It had caused her to put her past behind her. To go on with her life. To see Jeff as someone she could have a life with.

He came back to the room and she let him in, and together they unpacked the things they would need for the night, though Jeff had brought nothing with him. "When we get wherever we're going," he said quietly, "I'll call Jan and get her to send me some of my things."

"What will you do in the meantime?" she asked.

"Buy some things. I have my credit card. Tomorrow I'll buy a couple pairs of jeans and whatever else I need."

Leah sat down on the bed and pulled her feet beneath her. Her head dropped, and she traced a pattern on the bedspread with her finger. "I feel so guilty for doing this to you," she whispered. "I never wanted to cost you everything. That's what I tried so hard to avoid."

"Hey," he said, coming to sit across from her on the bed. "I get my daughter out of all this. That's a hell of a lot more than anything I left."

She looked up into his eyes—wishing, hoping that he would say that she was worth leaving it all for, too—and saw that the sadness and distrust she had read in his eyes so many times was lifting, but still there were a few shadows. He was still afraid to love her.

But she didn't need words or endearments from him. When he leaned over to kiss her, soft and sweet and unhurried, touching her face as if he couldn't fathom the softness of it, she realized she had everything she could ever hope for right here. Her baby safe and sound, and the man she loved sharing her bed.

As they made love, delightful images tiptoed through her mind. Images of white picket fences, and wisteria-covered arbors in the yard, and growing her own food, and making her own clothes, and being happy. Images of deep, long talks in the night with Jeff, of loving him with her body and soul, of hearing him say that he loved her.

He couldn't say it tonight, but he showed it, more than the first time when he had turned her away afterward, and even more than the second time when she had felt his barriers slipping. Tonight he loved with his whole being, with the part of him that was vulnerable to pain and heartache, the part of him that was still wounded from her own blade. He loved her without control, without inhibition, without despair. And she loved him in the same way.

They fell asleep in each other's arms, clinging lest one of them slipped away during the night. But the peace that blanketed them and protected them took away the fear, the paranoia, the distrust. They had each other, and they had Casey. And that was all either of them would ever need.

IT WAS 3:00 A. M. when they woke to a loud, urgent banging on their door, and clutching the blankets to them, they sprang up. Jeff grabbed his jeans and slipped them on. "What the hell?"

The pounding came again, louder, more frightening, and Casey sat up and began to cry. Leah tied the belt around her robe and grabbed Casey as Jeff started for the door.

"Open up!" someone shouted from outside.

"Who is it?" Jeff called.

"Police. Open the door."

Throwing a confused look back at Leah over his shoulder, Jeff opened the door. "Haven't you guys ever heard of plain old knocking? There's a baby in here—"

Three uniformed officers burst inside, and Casey screamed. Leah clutched the crying child to her and backed up against the wall.

"Jeff Hampton?" one of them asked.

"Yes."

"You're under arrest," the cop said.

"Arrest? For what?"

"For kidnapping. You have the right to remain silent...."

"Kidnapping? Who did I kidnap?"

"Miss Borgadeux and her daughter," the officer said, snapping cuffs on Jeff's wrists. "You have the right to an attorney...."

"No!" Leah rushed forward, trying to stop them from cuffing his hands. "It's not true. We came with him on our own. For heaven's sake, isn't anybody going to ask *me?*"

"You can make a statement at headquarters, Miss Borgadeux. Meanwhile, our orders are to take him in. He's a suspect in several other crimes, and we have to question him."

"Other crimes?" Jeff shouted. "What did Borgy tell you? That I'm a thief? A criminal? Is that what he told you?"

"That you'd kidnapped this child once before."

"*What?* He's the one—"

Two of the cops grabbed Jeff's arms and began escorting him out of the room. "If you cannot afford an attorney—"

"Stop, damn it!" Leah shouted. "You don't understand. He didn't kidnap us! Look at me! Why would I be defending him if I were being held against my will? Look at me!"

The two cops dragged Jeff out to the car, and the other one stopped in the doorway. "You can ride in the other squad car, Miss Borgadeux. We'll need you to make a statement."

"You bet I'll make a statement!" she cried. She ran to the door and watched as they manhandled Jeff into the back seat, and Casey began to scream louder.

"Daddy!"

"Jeff, don't worry!" Leah shouted across the parking lot. People began to open their doors, and a few dared to come out onto the landing and strained to see what was going on. "I'm coming, too. They won't get away with this."

"It's your father," he said before they closed the car door. "You know this is your father's doing."

"They can't hold you," she cried. "Any more than he can hold me!"

But she wasn't sure he heard, for as she shouted that out, the squad car he was in pulled away to take him to jail.

JEFF SAT in a questioning room under a glaring hot light as four officers who had nothing better to do surrounded him, staring at him as if he'd just committed a string of murders. They had brought him stale coffee, probably aged for the occasion, and the room was thick with smoke and bad breath.

"We can't let you go, pal, until you tell us what we need to know," the cop with the biggest mouth told him.

"You mean until I tell you what you want to hear, *pal*," Jeff returned. "I've already told you everything I know. I did not today, nor have I ever, kidnapped anyone. Lance Borgadeux, on the other hand, set up Casey's kidnapping, held his daughter against her will and set up this whole charade."

"He said you stole his car."

"His car? I haven't *touched* his car. Leah drove his car so she wouldn't get stopped at the gate of his estate. Otherwise, they would have hauled her back in." He leaned forward, beseeching the officers to pull some little thread of common sense from what was going on. "Think about it. Would she have to sneak off like that if she could come and go freely? And would she decide to run in the middle of the night?"

"So you didn't break into his home and abduct Miss Borgadeux and her daughter?"

"*My* daughter, and no, I did not. Leah called me to meet her, and I did."

"At which time you forced her into your car and headed north?"

Jeff rubbed his weary face and began to laugh mirthlessly. "Do you guys not speak English or what? She was going to leave alone. She was going to go so far he'd never find her. I decided to go with her. Why don't you just ask her?"

One of the cops who'd come into the room late—presumably because he was questioning Leah—stood up and nodded toward the others. "Story checks out. She backs it up a hundred percent. We can't really book him under the circumstances."

"If you want to book someone, book Borgadeux," Jeff said. "The man needs to be taken off the streets. He's dangerous."

The big-mouthed cop stood up. "We're letting you go, but we'll be watching you, Hampton. I'm not totally convinced you're without blame in all this."

Jeff scraped his chair back and got up. "I don't care what you're totally convinced of. Now, if you'll excuse me, I want to go see if my fiancée and my daughter are all right."

"Fiancée?"

Jeff locked eyes with the man who'd caused him the most trouble in this ordeal. "Yes, fiancée. Tell Borgadeux that, *pal*. Tell him I'm going to marry his daughter. This time he isn't going to stop me."

MORNING HAD DAWNED before Leah and Jeff stepped out of the precinct, carrying the sleeping child, and rode back to their room in a cab, since they both refused to accept a ride in the squad car.

When they had been returned to their hotel room, exhausted and so angry that neither of them was able to sleep, they began to pack.

Leah looked at Jeff and came up behind him. She touched his back and laid her face against it. "Jeff, I'm so sorry he did this. I'm so sorry that it keeps falling on you."

"He's got to be stopped," he whispered. "We can't go on like this."

She felt him pulling away from her, changing his mind about wanting to go through all this with her, about all the sacrifices he was making. And she didn't blame him.

Taking a deep breath, he turned around and took her arms, making her look up at him. "Leah, we have to talk," he said quietly.

Tears came to her eyes, but she tried to blink them back. Gently she took his hands, brought them to her mouth. "You're having second thoughts," she whispered. "I understand, Jeff. Really I do."

He nodded. "I'm having second thoughts, all right, but not about us. Not about you."

"What then?"

"I had a lot of time to think when they had me in there," he said. "And I decided that there's no way I can let him control us this way. We're letting him send us running blindly. We're letting him take everything we have. We're letting him manipulate us again."

"But what else can we do? He could take Casey, make up lies about you, set you up again, ruin both of us."

"No. Not if we let him know that we're more than ready to expose him and prosecute him. Not if we stand up to him."

"You want to go back." It was a statement, steeped in disappointment and apprehension. It was a statement steeped in fear.

"Yes. I want to confront him, Leah. I have to do this. It's right."

Leah looked over to the bed where Casey slept as they packed. She wondered if all the turmoil was doing harm to her little spirit, or if she really took things in stride, as she appeared to. "But if he would have Casey kidnapped, and you arrested—"

"Now we know what we're dealing with, Leah. We'll make sure that he never sees Casey again. *I'll* make sure."

Her tears fell over her lashes, trickled down her cheeks. "I'm scared, Jeff."

"I'm scared, too," he whispered. "But I'm scared of what will happen if we don't stop him. I'm scared of what will become of us if we let him manipulate us." It was his turn to take her hands and folding them in his, he pressed them to his chest. "Leah, the year after you left me was the worst kind of agony. I learned to be numb after that, and it's taken me a long time to trust anyone again. But I feel myself trusting you again."

She slid her arms around his waist, laid her head against his chest as he continued. He cupped his hand over her head, began to stroke her hair. "Maybe it took seeing how low your father would sink to make me believe what you must have been going through when you left me before. Maybe I'm just starting to see that you really had no choices."

A sigh of relief escaped her lungs. "Oh, Jeff, I couldn't let you lose everything you had worked for because of me."

He tilted her face up, looked hard and deep into her eyes. When he spoke, his voice was cracked. "Nothing he could have taken from me would have hurt as bad as losing you, Leah. Nothing.''

She sucked in a sob and tried to stop the quivering of her lips. He lowered his face and kissed away one of her tears. ''I love you, Leah. I still love you. I guess somewhere, under all the anger, I always have.''

She tightened her embrace, and he held her with the strength and determination of the only person who had the power to save her.

Slowly he pulled back so that he could look into her eyes. ''We have to go back,'' he said. ''I can't walk away and let that man win. I can't walk away after he destroyed our relationship, had my baby kidnapped, had me arrested.... Please understand, Leah. I have to confront him, once and for all. It's the only way you and I will ever have a happy future together.''

The word ''future'' fell upon her heart like warm sunlight on a snow-covered lawn. ''All right, Jeff. We'll go back.''

''We'll go today,'' he said. ''I'll take you to my parents'. We'll spend the night there, and tomorrow you and Casey can wait there while I confront your father. While I tell him how it's going to be.''

''Your parents won't like it,'' she whispered. ''Having me around. They'll hate it.''

''It'll be okay. Sooner or later, things will be clearer to them.''

THE MOMENT THEY PULLED onto the gravel drive at his parents' house that night, Florence and Al Hampton rushed out to the car.

"Where have you been?" his mother cried, bursting into tears.

"They said you had kidnapped Casey and Leah. And that awful man, that Lance Borgadeux, has been harassing us with his phone calls and his thugs—"

"I'm sorry, Mom. I didn't mean to worry you." Jeff hugged his mother, then his father, and turned back to the car to help Leah and Casey out. "It's just that we left suddenly."

"What the hell is going on?" his father demanded.

Leah clutched Casey tighter to her and faced his parents. "Mr. and Mrs. Hampton, if there were rumors, my father started them."

"They weren't just rumors. They were news reports, in the newspaper, no less! Jeff, you should have never gotten tied up with that family. It's poison!"

"Stop it."

Jeff stepped closer to Leah, took Casey from her and set his free arm protectively around her. "Leah's as much a victim as I am. Borgadeux set up the kidnapping himself so he could manipulate Leah. As soon as we figured it out, we decided to put ourselves as far from him as we could."

"But he still had Jeff arrested in Fort Walton Beach," Leah added. "He'll go to any lengths."

His parents looked stricken. "He had his own grandchild kidnapped?" His mother turned her teary eyes on her son. "And you were in jail? Are you all right? Oh, my God, *he's* the one who should be locked up!"

"He won't get away with it," Jeff assured his parents. "We need for you to let us stay here tonight. Tomorrow, I'm going back to Tampa to confront him, and Dad, I need for you to protect Leah and Casey. I'm counting on you."

"But what about you? Who's going to protect you from him?"

"I can take care of myself," he said. "I have ammunition now. I have enough on him to prosecute, but he won't want that."

"You will prosecute, won't you?"

Leah gave him a dreadful look.

"We don't know yet," Jeff said. "We don't want Casey marked forever. What we really want is just to be left alone. Just for him to get out of our lives. If I have anything to say about it, that man will never see either his daughter or his granddaughter again."

Both parents gave Leah an assessing look—a look that said they still didn't trust her, they still didn't like her and they still could not accept her into their family. But it was a tentative look, one that offered the slightest hope that they might be wrong.

They went into the house and got Casey settled into bed. Since he didn't want to upset his mother further by sharing a bed with Leah, she was sleeping with Casey that night.

"Don't worry about me tomorrow, okay?" he whispered, holding her tightly against him before he left her for the night.

"I won't," she whispered. "I just wish your parents didn't hate having me here so much."

"They'll come around," he said. "In time, they'll love you, too. Remember, we have all the time in the world."

"Do we?" she asked. "Because to me, it seems like we just have a few more hours."

"He's not going to ruin us again," he whispered. "I promise you, this will all be over tomorrow."

Chapter Twelve

Leah and Casey were the first ones up the next morning, for Jeff's parents slept late since they always stayed so late at the bar. Casey, who didn't care where she was, popped up at the crack of dawn with a man's appetite.

Setting Casey up on the counter, Leah began quietly moving around the Hamptons' kitchen, trying to find Casey something to eat without waking anyone.

"There's cereal in the pantry." Leah turned and saw Florence in the kitchen doorway, looking at her with that drawn, reluctant expression. "Here, I'll get it."

"Thanks. I hope we didn't wake you. Casey never sleeps late."

"I'll never mind waking up to my granddaughter's voice," Florence said, softening as she picked Casey up. "Where's Jeff?"

"Still sleeping, I guess. I made coffee if you want some."

For a few minutes, they worked quietly, only speaking to Casey as they prepared her breakfast, passing each other with "excuse me's" and "sorry's."

Finally, Casey was eating and there was nothing left to do. Leah gave Florence a tentative look. "Will you sit down with us? Have some coffee?"

Looking trapped, Florence poured herself a cup and sat down, fixing her eyes on Casey.

"Look, Mrs. Hampton, I know how you feel about me, and I can't blame you. But I really appreciate you letting us stay here."

"Casey," she corrected. "I'm letting Casey stay. You're just here because you happen to be her mother."

The sting hit its mark, and Leah swallowed and tried to start again. "I realize that."

She took a deep breath and looked down at her coffee, as if some answers would materialize on the obsidian surface. "You know, when I left Jeff before, it wasn't because I wanted to. It was because of the kind of man my father is. The kind of man who could ruin Jeff if I didn't do what he wanted. You must see that now, after all he's done."

"All I see, Leah, is that you've brought nothing but heartache and despair and turmoil into my son's life." The words were spoken calmly, gently, but the bite of them was devastating. She sipped her coffee, pushed Casey's hair back from her face and looked at Leah again. "Leah, I know that it may not have been your fault. But the fact is, you hurt him deeply before, and now, finding out that you've deliberately kept his daughter from him ... I just don't know if I can ever forgive you for that."

"I don't know if he'll ever forgive me, either," she whispered. "I don't even know if I can forgive myself. All I know, Mrs. Hampton, is that I still love him with all my heart, and if there were even a remote possibility that he would give me another chance, I would make it up to him. And to you. You'd see."

"But second chances are hard to come by, Leah. And to be perfectly honest, I don't think he *should* give you one."

Through the tears clouding her eyes, Leah noticed a movement in the doorway, and she looked up to see Jeff standing there, his face a mask of controlled anger.

Blinking back her tears, she whispered, "Good morning."

"Is it?" he asked, his eyes settling on his mother.

Florence slid her chair back. "I'll get you some coffee."

He came farther into the room as his mother went for the coffee and sat down next to Leah. Their eyes met for a moment, and she knew he saw her tears. Feeling awkward, clumsy, silly, she scooted her chair back. "Can you watch Casey, Jeff? I'll be right back."

He nodded, and quickly she left the room.

His eyes followed her until she was gone, and he felt his heart sink for the pain she was feeling. He wanted to stop it, to heal it, as she had started the healing within him.

His mother brought his coffee cup to the table and sat down across from him. "I was just telling Leah that—"

"I heard what you told her, Mom," he said. "And now I have something to tell you."

He saw her stiffen, saw her take a deep breath and hold it, bracing herself.

"I don't think it's up to you to decide whether or not I give Leah a second chance. It's between her and me. And as for you accepting her, that's up to you. I'm not accepted by her father, and that's just fine with me. We can live without your acceptance, too, if we have to."

"What are you talking about?" his mother demanded. "Are you going to get back together with her?"

He looked down at his hands, studied them, then clasped them on the table. "I'm in love with her, Mom. She's the only woman I've ever felt this way about. Yes, she's dragged me through hell, but she went there, too. She had more of it than I did."

Casey looked up at them, her eyes widening at the sharper tones in their voices, and Florence waited for a moment before answering. Trying to smile a shaky smile, she poured Casey some more cereal.

Softening her tone, she said, "I want you to be happy, Jeff. That's all. Is that such a bad thing for a mother to want for her son?"

"Leah makes me happy, Mom. Since she walked out on me, I've been miserable. Now she's back, and I feel like my life has started over again. She gave me Casey, and I want to give her the family she never had. I want you to love her, too."

"That'll take time," she said, taking his hand. "But if that's the way you feel, son, I'll do my best."

WHEN CASEY HAD EATEN her fill, Florence took her outside to see the litter of kittens, and Jeff went to Leah's bedroom. "Leah?" he called quietly through the door.

"Come in."

He opened the door, stepped tentatively inside. She had been crying harder, and her nose and lips were red with the strain of it. But she had wiped her eyes dry so that she could hold up that brave front—that front she had been born to wear.

"Are you all right?"

"Sure, fine," she said, turning away from him and busying herself folding Casey's clothes. "Where's Casey?"

"She went out to see the kittens with Mom. She's warming up to her."

"Yeah," she said. "She doesn't scream when I'm not around anymore. Kind of amazing, with all that's been going on. I guess kids are more resilient than we give them credit for."

He stepped closer and reached out to still her hands. She looked at him, and he saw the tears forming again. "I talked to my mother," he whispered.

"About what?" Her lips quivered with the effort of not crying.

"About you. About us."

"Us?" Her voice was shaky, unsteady.

"Yes. I told her, Leah, that I'm in love with you."

Those tears she struggled so hard to hold back splashed onto her cheeks, and her eyebrows lifted in disbelief. "You did?"

"Yes, I did," he whispered, framing her face and wiping a tear with his thumb.

She sucked in a breath and covered her mouth with her hand. "And what did she say?"

He smiled. "She promised to go easier on you."

He pulled her against him, buried his face in her hair and felt his own eyes stinging with emotion as she wept into his shirt. "I'm sorry she hurt you."

"She was just being honest," she said. "She had every right."

He lifted her face to his, met her lips and pulled her into a kiss so deep she would have gladly drowned in it. But he was there to breathe life back into her, passing his strength through the gentleness of his touch, carrying the burden of love and loneliness she had carried alone for so long.

When the kiss ended on a sigh, he threaded his fingers through her hair and pressed his mouth against her temple. "I've got to go," he said, reminding her of the dread that had kept her awake all night. "It's time to confront your father."

"I want to come with you," she said. "I want to be there."

"No."

"Jeff, please. It's my battle...."

"It's *our* battle. Besides, Casey would fall apart if she didn't know you were nearby. And it could get ugly. There's no reason for you to be in the middle of it."

"But I *am* in the middle of it."

"Please," he said. "Let me do this. It's very important to me."

Seeing that his mind couldn't be changed, she nodded quietly. "All right, I'll stay. Just be careful, Jeff. I don't think he would hurt you physically, but I didn't think he'd kidnap Casey, either. Please be careful."

"I promise," he said, slipping out of her arms. "I'll be back in a little while, and then we'll have some plans to make."

Leah choked back a new surge of tears as he left her there.

FROM THE WAY Borgy's staff buzzed around him, one would have thought Jeff was a fugitive from the law who had finally come to turn himself in. Borgy's secretary dropped a stack of papers she was holding as she reached for the telephone to buzz her boss. A cluster of security men, or "thugs" as his mother had called them, immediately appeared in the room outside Borgy's office. And the man himself appeared in less than thirty seconds after Jeff announced who he was.

"Where's my daughter?" Borgy shouted, his voice shaking the very walls of his office. "What have you done with her?"

"In the office, Borgy," Jeff said, breaking loose from the security guard's grip. "This is just between you and me. No bodyguards, no detectives, no cops. Just you and me in the office. You wouldn't like it if they heard what I have to say."

"I have no secrets from my staff," Borgy said, but his imperial tone had slipped a note.

"Oh no?" Jeff asked. "Then I guess they'll all go to jail with you, Borgy. I mean, if they knew what you were doing—"

"Jail?" His secretary came to her feet, staring at Borgadeux.

Jeff saw his face redden.

"I don't know what you're talking about."

"I'd be happy to elaborate," Jeff obliged. "Since everyone knows and all...."

Borgadeux flung open the door to his office and gestured for Jeff to go in.

"Great idea," Jeff said, slipping his hands into his pockets and ambling into the elaborate nerve center of Borgadeux Enterprises.

He walked to the middle of the carpet, turned and watched Borgy follow him in and close the double doors behind him. His face was still crimson when he turned around.

"I warn you," Borgadeux said. "You're in a hell of a lot more danger with me alone than you would be in front of witnesses."

"Oh, I don't doubt that you're dangerous, Borgy," Jeff said, holding his cold stare. "But I'm the one who was in jail yesterday. At the moment, I'm more dangerous than you are."

A vein at Borgadeux's temple pulsed as he crossed the room toward Jeff. "Where's my daughter?"

"She's not in Fort Walton Beach waiting to bail me out, if that's what you hoped," he said. "And she's not talking to the DA about the fact that her own father had his granddaughter kidnapped."

The surprise on Borgy's face was worth every moment of anger and rage Jeff had experienced. "What did you say?"

Jeff grinned. "We know, Borgy. I have my own detectives, and really, it doesn't take a genius to figure out what you've done and why."

"Are you accusing me of—"

"Yes. I'm accusing you of hiring strangers to kidnap my daughter so that you could manipulate yours. I'm accusing you of harassing and terrorizing and threatening Leah so that you could get her back under your control."

"You must be crazy! Why would I do something like that? I would never—"

"You did it, and we can prove it." The words were so calm, so unemotional, that Borgy only stared at him. Jeff picked up a framed photo of Leah and Casey, looked at it and set it back down. "Now, as I see it, Borgy, we have a few options. My preference is the one where I expose you for what you are and turn you over to the DA, and stand back and watch while they cuff you and haul you off to jail like they did to me. But that's only second to the one where I take you on myself and tear you limb from limb until I have satisfaction that you've gotten what you deserve…which is to live in the same kind of hell you've put Leah through."

Borgadeux's shoulders stiffened, and his hard expression held firm, not cracking. "The DA is a friend of mine. He would never believe you."

"Oh, he'd believe me," Jeff assured him. "And you couldn't keep it quiet, Borgy, not with it all over the news. Hell, it just might ruin you."

He paced across the room, stopped at a pair of bronze baby shoes displayed on a marble shelf, saw the inscription of Leah's name and birth date. Borgadeux waited, solid and expressionless, holding his breath. "But Leah and I have opted for something else entirely," Jeff said finally.

"What?"

"Well, Leah wanted to move to another town where you'd never find her again. Someplace where she didn't have to look over her shoulder for fear her father's thugs would snatch her daughter to manipulate her. Someplace where they could live in peace. I was glad to take her to that place. That's where we were headed when you had me arrested like a drug lord in the middle of the night. And that kind of got me thinking."

"Get to the point, Hampton. I'm not a patient man."

"And neither am I," Jeff said, squaring off with the man across from him. "Which is why I decided that I can't let you get away with this. You aren't going to run Leah away from her home and her business, you aren't going to force us to uproot our daughter, and by God, you aren't going to ruin me the way you threatened Leah you would. You're not going to do a damned thing, because if you do, I'll smear your name so bad that you'll be happy to wind up in jail."

The vein in Borgy's temple twitched, but his expression did not change.

"The fact is that I'm still in love with Leah," Jeff said. "And I'm going to marry her. I'm going to move her and Casey into my house, and we're going to be happy there. And if you ever come within a hundred feet of my wife or my child, I'll splatter your ass all over the newspapers and television screens for as far as they know your name, and then I'll take my family so far away that it'll be like they never existed. Have you got that?"

For the first time, the man's hard facade began to crack. "Hampton, whatever I did, it was in the best interest of my daughter. She knows that—"

Venomous rage bled into Jeff's eyes as he came within inches of the man. "I know that you are capable of horrible things, Borgy. I'm going to document every bit of my proof and keep it locked up where I can pull it out any time I need it. You just never know when the mood might strike me to do you in. You just never know."

When the telephone rang at the Hamptons', Leah fought the urge to spring for it. It wasn't her house, she reminded herself as Florence answered in the kitchen. If Jeff wanted to speak to her, he'd have to go through his mother first.

But it wasn't Jeff, she gathered the moment Florence stepped into the dining room where she and Casey sat putting together Lego pieces.

"It's your father," Florence said. "Do you want me to tell him you're not here?"

An alarm went off in her heart, and she tried to think, tried to put together broken images of what might have happened to make him call here. Had Jeff reached him yet? Had something happened to him? Had her father hurt him?

She raked a hand through her hair and came slowly to her feet. "Did...did he say if Jeff's been there yet?"

"No," Florence said. "He's very rude and obnoxious, and he just demanded to talk to you. I can hang up on him if you want—"

"No." She swallowed and reached for the phone. "It might be about Jeff. I'll take it."

Florence sat down next to Casey as Leah put the phone to her ear, and Leah could see from the disapproval on her face that she expected Leah to defect to her father's side of this fight again. "Hello?"

"Leah, he's filling your head full of lies, sweetheart. He's brainwashing you. You've got to get out of there—"

"Shut up!" The harsh words startled both Florence and Casey but not as much as they startled Borgadeux. "Just shut up!" she shouted again. "You're the one who tried to brainwash me!"

"Leah, I'm your father! I love you!"

"You don't know what love is!" she shouted back. "Love is not fear, and it's not intimidation. It's not lying and stealing and hurting!"

"I never hurt you, Leah. I would never have hurt you or the baby!"

"You let your lowlifes take my baby!" she screamed. "You watched me die a little at a time! And it was all so you could have your almighty power!"

"Leah, this is crazy. We've got to meet somewhere, darling. We've got to talk."

"Not without a team of reporters with television cameras, a battalion of cops and the DA," Leah said. "Still want to talk, Dad?"

Borgy's voice faltered, and she could hear that he wept. Oddly, she felt no sympathy for the man. "He told me I could never see you again," Borgy said. "Don't you understand that I can't accept that? You're all I have, Leah."

"Then you have nothing," she said. "Jeff meant every word he said about turning you in if you ever come near us again. I'm getting a gun, Dad, and I'm going to learn how to use it. And I'll do whatever I have to to protect myself and my daughter. Even from you."

Without waiting for her father's response, she slammed down the phone. Florence stood up, and the look on her face revealed that she was letting down the barriers. She opened her arms for Leah, and wilting like a delicate flower too long in the heat, Leah fell into her embrace and cried until her tears ran out.

LEAH WAS WAITING OUTSIDE on the front porch with Florence and Casey when Jeff drove up, and Florence took her hand. "No obvious cuts or bruises," she said. "Guess he's all right."

Leah gave her a smile that was full of gratitude, a smile that thanked her for opening her arms to her, for seeing her true colors at last, for accepting that she was someone who deserved a chance. "I'll go see."

She ran down the steps to the car as Jeff was getting out. "Are you okay? He didn't hurt you?"

Jeff laughed. "Of course not. He was so scared, he wouldn't have touched me."

"I know," she said. "He called here."

"He *what?*" Jeff's smile crashed, and his face resumed the murderous expression with which he had confronted Borgadeux. As if to fulfill that rage, he started to get back in the car. "I *warned* him to leave you alone. I'll kill him."

"Wait!" Leah cried, pulling him back out. "I handled it, Jeff. I told him I was getting a gun."

Jeff turned back to her. His breathing was heavier as he waited for a reason not to go after the man again. "What did he say to that?"

"What *could* he say? I think he knew it was the end when you told him, but he had to hear it from me."

Florence came up beside them, holding Casey on her hip. "You would have been proud of her, Jeff, the way she told him off. She really let him have it, and there's nothing I like better than a good fighter."

Jeff seemed to relax, and he set his arm across Leah's shoulders, as if to feel for himself that Borgy hadn't done her more harm. Then, as if he only now recognized the significance of what his mother had said, he passed a questioning look from Leah to his mother. "Did I miss something?"

Waving him off, Florence turned him around and gave him a quick once-over. "Are you sure he left you in one piece? Didn't even try to cripple you?"

"That's not his style," Jeff said, still frowning. "It's too obvious. He likes doing things the underhanded way. But I think he's the one who's been crippled. He's losing Leah and Casey for good."

"His loss is our gain," Florence said. She started back up to the house.

Jeff stood still, a slow smile dawning across his face. "Did she say what I thought she said?"

Leah smiled. "Your mother and I are going to get along just fine," she said. "Come on. Let's get our stuff and go home."

LATE THAT NIGHT, when they were back in Jeff's home and Casey slept soundly in her room, Leah lay on the couch, cocooned in his arms.

"There's one thing I told your father that I haven't told you, yet," he whispered, gazing into her eyes and fingering her hair.

She looked up at him and touched his face, wondering at the texture of the stubble across his chin, the angle of his jaw, the shape of his chin. "What?"

"I told him..." He swallowed, and moved his mouth to her fingertips, caught one in his mouth. His eyes met hers as he laced his fingers through hers, bathed each tip and traced the pad of her thumb across his lip. "I told him I was going to marry you."

Their eyes locked softly, foreign beacons meeting across a night sky—his apprehensive, hers stunned. "You did?"

"Yes," he whispered. "Maybe I should have asked you first, but—"

"No." She got up on her knees and looked down at the face she loved. Her eyes were misty, soft, vulnerable as they beheld him. "It's...it's all right. If you meant it."

"I meant it." Releasing her, he reached into his pocket and pulled out the small velvet box he had put there the moment he'd come home. He had waited until Casey was asleep, until they could be alone, and over and over he had slipped his hand in his pocket and felt it against his fingers, a reassurance that the light wouldn't die the moment his happiness blossomed fully. "I didn't mean to tell him first. What I really wanted to do..."

Leah's eyes fell to the box, the box he had offered her once before. She had never been able to take it, for her father had already drawn the lines. Now, knowing what was inside that box that she had never dreamed he'd kept, her eyes filled with tears. "Jeff?"

His hands shook as he lifted the lid, and Leah saw the diamond ring she had wanted so badly to wear the first time. It had dazzled her then, as it did now, and she knew it had been way more than he could afford when he'd bought it. "You kept it," she whispered.

"Yeah," he said. "If I had taken it back, they would have sold it to someone else. I couldn't stand the thought of anyone else ever wearing it but you." He took it out of the box and reached for her hand.

"Leah," he whispered, "I love you more than you could ever imagine. I don't ever want to face the thought of losing you again. I want to live with you for the rest of my life." His own eyes filled with half-moons of tears as he breathed out the words. "Will you be my wife?"

Her tears rolled down her cheeks as she pressed her forehead against his. "I love you, Jeff Hampton," she said. "And I've never wanted anything more in my life than to be your wife."

He slipped the ring on her finger, brought the finger to his lips. Closing his eyes, he kissed her knuckle, then moved her hand against his cheek. "I wanted to marry you the first day I met you...." His eyes opened and he framed her face and caught her lips. "I wanted to marry you the day you left me...." He slid his hands down her neck and pulled her against him. "And I want to marry you now. I want to love you forever and make you the happiest woman on earth."

"You've already made me the happiest woman on earth," she said. "Now just make me your wife."

Their loving was slow, selfless, sensitive, as each moved to prove how deep their love was. And as they came together in a union more perfect than either had experienced before, they knew that nothing would ever come between them again. They were solid, they were whole.

They were one.

Epilogue

"Hurry, Mommy! Daddy'll be home soon."

Leah smiled at Casey and took the three strands of Christmas tree lights from her. It was going to be a surprise for Jeff. Casey had seen the "invisible Christmas tree" at the mall, made of lights coming from a center point and angling out to the ground. She had been fascinated that it looked like nothing but wires and bulbs when the lights were off, but when the strings were plugged in, it became a glorious display that lit up the building. She had convinced Leah to make one in the center of their front yard.

To the child, it was a miracle, making something magnificent out of a mess of tangled wires. To Leah, it was more than a miracle. It was a symbol of the beautiful union she and Jeff had created in marriage.

The door to the house opened, and Jan stuck her head out. "Hey, Leah! Mom's on the phone and wants to know if you want lace or ribbon to edge that baby blanket she's making."

Leah got to her feet and, smiling, set her hand over her swollen stomach where her and Jeff's baby continuously made his presence known. "Tell her, ribbon. Yellow or white." She felt the baby kick as if in protest, then shook her head. "Never mind. Tell her I'll call her back."

Jan waved and retreated back inside, where she had engaged in hanging the decorations she and Leah had found at a craft fair that morning. They had saved the tree-trimming for Jeff to help with, but the rest would be a surprise.

Leah turned back to the "invisible tree" and saw that Casey was tangled up in the two remaining strings. "Casey! What are you doing?"

"I can do it myself," she said. "I'm big."

"Not that big." She stooped down and began trying to untangle her.

"Plug me in, Mommy! Let's see if I look like a tree!"

"We have enough trees around here, thank you." She stood up and stretched out the strand and stapled it to the plywood on the ground. "There. Almost finished."

"Who's that, Mommy?"

Leah stood up, dusting off her knees and saw a black limousine coming through the gates that she had forgotten to close after she and Jan got home. A skein of fear shot through her. "Come here, Casey."

She picked up the three-year-old and, holding her close, stood motionless as the limo approached.

"Is that Daddy?"

"No, honey."

The car came to a halt, and Leah felt the blood drain from her face as her father got out of the car.

She hadn't seen him in a year, and the age and weathering of his face surprised her. She hadn't expected these months to do so much damage.

"Leah." The word, broken and soft, made her back away.

"I don't want you here," she said. "I told you—"

"Please, Leah." He burst into tears and held up his hands. "I've given you a year. I haven't contacted you once. But you're my daughter, and it's Christmas."

Afraid that his emotional state was upsetting Casey, she set her down. "Run in, Casey. Aunt Jan needs your help."

Casey didn't move.

Borgadeux bent over and started to pick her up.

"Put her down!" The words came too harshly and Casey started to cry. Reaching out, she took her away from him. "Don't you ever touch my daughter again."

"Leah, I wouldn't hurt her! She's my grandchild!"

"You had her kidnapped! You let people who commit crimes for money take my baby for an entire day. How dare you say that you wouldn't hurt her?"

"I've paid!" His tears came harder, and his big, slumped shoulders shook. "I've learned. All I ever wanted was to keep you close to me. I didn't know any other way to do that. Instead, I drove you away."

He broke down, and Leah only stared at him, unable to lift a hand to comfort him.

THE LIMO WAS THE FIRST thing Jeff saw as he came up the drive, and he felt his heart rate shift into high gear. He saw Borgadeux standing with Leah, and Casey between them.

Throwing the car into Park, he got out and bolted toward the man, ready to beat him to a pulp, ready to call out all the legal dogs he could find, ready to make good on his threat.

"I warned you, Borgy—"

The man turned around, and the tears and wrinkles and age on the man's face stopped Jeff. "I'm going," he said, like a defeated, broken old man. "But I had to come. I had to try."

Jeff stepped close to Leah, set a possessive arm around her, and touched Casey's shoulder as if the mere touch could protect her from the debilitating love of this man who was her grandfather.

"I don't blame you for hating me," Borgadeux told him. "I'm responsible for more pain than any man should have to suffer. But if it's any consolation, I've suffered, too."

"It is," Jeff said.

Slowly Borgadeux turned back to the car, opened the back door and looked around the yard at the newly hung Christmas decorations, the swing set on the side of the house, the sandbox. He looked at Casey, plump and healthy and full of life. And then he looked at his daughter, standing silently beside her husband, her belly full with the new life they had created together.

"I've been a fool," he whispered. "Maybe someday you'll find it in your heart to give me another chance."

Jeff held Leah as she watched her father get back into his limo and ride out of sight.

IN THE WEE HOURS of morning when the night wind sang its doleful song against the corners of the house and the full moon lit the window, Jeff woke to an empty bed and found Leah sitting on the windowsill, staring out into the darkness.

"You okay?" he asked, sitting up.

She smiled. "The baby was doing gymnastics and woke me," she said. "He'll be the world's first infant gold medalist."

Jeff scooted onto the sill behind her and reached around her, feeing her stomach with both hands. "Feels quiet in there to me. Are you sure something else isn't bothering you?"

"Like what?"

"Like your father?" He rested his chin on her shoulder and nuzzled his face against hers.

"I don't know," she whispered. "It's all so confusing. I thought I hated him, and then today when I saw him, he looked so old and so alone—"

"And you felt sorry for him."

"I don't know what I felt," she said, leaning back against him.

They were quiet for a while, staring out into the night, listening to the wind and relaxing in the warmth of their love. Finally Leah spoke again.

"If I hadn't had a second chance," she whispered, "I wouldn't be here with you. Maybe everyone—no matter how cruel or hateful—maybe everyone deserves a second chance."

For a long time Jeff was still, his face pressed against hers and his hands cupping her stomach. After a while, a slow sigh escaped him, and he dropped his hands, releasing her.

She sat up straight and turned around as he stood up. "Jeff?"

Quietly he walked across the room, got the telephone and brought it back to her. "Ten to one he couldn't sleep tonight, either."

Leah took the phone and stared at it, unable to believe what he suggested. "You want me to call him?"

He touched her face and tipped it up to his. "If you need to. If he's left an empty hole inside you, Leah, then I think it needs to be filled."

She looked at the phone again, an uncertain frown tugging at her brows. "I don't know, Jeff. The things he's done.... We've had such a good life this past year. I don't want him to spoil it."

"Leah, look at me." She looked up at him again, saw the face that had at last taken away her insecurities, the face that meant everything to her. "We've built something too strong for him to knock down again. He can't hurt us now. Go ahead and call him if you need to."

Leah pulled him into her arms and kissed him with the gratitude and love he had cultivated in her so carefully over the last year, for he had taught her the true value of second chances. And as he turned her around in his arms and pulled her back against him, holding her, she smiled...and began to dial her father's number.

PENNY JORDAN

Sins and infidelities...
Dreams and obsessions...
Shattering secrets
unfold in...

THE HIDDEN YEARS

SAGE — stunning, sensual and vibrant, she spent a lifetime distancing herself from a past too painful to confront... the mother who seemed to hold her at bay, the father who resented her and the heartache of unfulfilled love. To the world, Sage was independent and invulnerable— but it was a mask she cultivated to hide a desperation she herself couldn't quite understand... until an unforeseen turn of events drew her into the discovery of the hidden years, finally allowing Sage to open her heart to a passion denied for so long.

The Hidden Years—a compelling novel of truth and passion that will unlock the heart and soul of every woman.

AVAILABLE IN OCTOBER!
Watch for your opportunity to complete your Penny Jordan set.
POWER PLAY and SILVER will also be available in October.

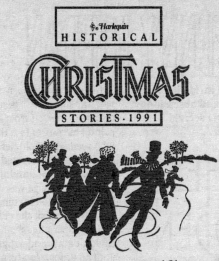

H A R L E Q U I N
American Romance®

COMING NEXT MONTH

#413 CHASING TROUBLE by Anne Stuart

San Francisco heiress Sally MacArthur knew she needed to hire a hard-boiled detective to find her half sister Lucy, who had run off with a mobster. Sally expected an adventure when she joined private investigator James Diamond but she didn't expect to find a diamond in the rough.

#414 RACING WITH THE MOON by Muriel Jensen

Genny Scott had a secret she'd guarded her entire life. Even her young daughter didn't know what she lived with from day to day. When Jack Fleming, a man determined to capture her heart, found out the truth, he surprised Genny with an interesting proposition. And for once in her life she didn't know what to do....

#415 RUNNING ON EMPTY by Kay Wilding

Elizabeth Bartlett, the bank president's daughter, and Cal Potts, the bad boy from the wrong side of the tracks, had shared a forbidden love as teens. Ten years later, Elizabeth discovered that coming back home is never easy, especially when old flames still burn.

#416 HOME IN HIS ARMS by Suzanne Simmons Guntrum

Jessie Jordan couldn't shake the feeling that she'd met Mitch Jade before. But the gentle Quaker and the fiery reporter were strangers ... until destiny brought them together in a single, explosive moment that would change them forever.

Take 4 bestselling love stories FREE
Plus get a FREE surprise gift!

HARLEQUIN®
OFFICIAL SWEEPSTAKES RULES

NO PURCHASE NECESSARY

1. To enter, complete an Official Entry Form or 3"× 5" index card by hand-printing, in plain block letters, your complete name, address, phone number and age, and mailing it to: Harlequin Fashion A Whole New You Sweepstakes, P.O. Box 9056, Buffalo, NY 14269-9056.

   No responsibility is assumed for lost, late or misdirected mail. Entries must be sent separately with first class postage affixed, and be received no later than December 31, 1991 for eligibility.

2. Winners will be selected by D.L. Blair, Inc., an independent judging organization whose decisions are final, in random drawings to be held on January 30, 1992 in Blair, NE at 10:00 a.m. from among all eligible entries received.

3. The prizes to be awarded and their approximate retail values are as follows: Grand Prize — A brand-new Mercury Sable LS plus a trip for two (2) to Paris, including round-trip air transportation, six (6) nights hotel accommodation, a $1,400 meal/spending money stipend and $2,000 cash toward a new fashion wardrobe (approximate value: $28,000) or $15,000 cash; two (2) Second Prizes — A trip to Paris, including round-trip air transportation, six (6) nights hotel accommodation, a $1,400 meal/spending money stipend and $2,000 cash toward a new fashion wardrobe (approximate value: $11,000) or $5,000 cash; three (3) Third Prizes — $2,000 cash toward a new fashion wardrobe. All prizes are valued in U.S. currency. Travel award air transportation is from the commercial airport nearest winner's home. Travel is subject to space and accommodation availability, and must be completed by June 30, 1993. Sweepstakes offer is open to residents of the U.S. and Canada who are 21 years of age or older as of December 31, 1991, except residents of Puerto Rico, employees and immediate family members of Torstar Corp., its affiliates, subsidiaries, and all agencies, entities and persons connected with the use, marketing, or conduct of this sweepstakes. All federal, state, provincial, municipal and local laws apply. Offer void wherever prohibited by law. Taxes and/or duties, applicable registration and licensing fees, are the sole responsibility of the winners. Any litigation within the province of Quebec respecting the conduct and awarding of a prize may be submitted to the Régie des loteries et courses du Québec. All prizes will be awarded; winners will be notified by mail. No substitution of prizes is permitted.

4. Potential winners must sign and return any required Affidavit of Eligibility/Release of Liability within 30 days of notification. In the event of noncompliance within this time period, the prize may be awarded to an alternate winner. Any prize or prize notification returned as undeliverable may result in the awarding of that prize to an alternate winner. By acceptance of their prize, winners consent to use of their names, photographs or their likenesses for purposes of advertising, trade and promotion on behalf of Torstar Corp. without further compensation. Canadian winners must correctly answer a time-limited arithmetical question in order to be awarded a prize.

5. For a list of winners (available after 3/31/92), send a separate stamped, self-addressed envelope to: Harlequin Fashion A Whole New You Sweepstakes, P.O. Box 4694, Blair, NE 68009.

PREMIUM OFFER TERMS

To receive your gift, complete the Offer Certificate according to directions. Be certain to enclose the required number of "Fashion A Whole New You" proofs of product purchase (which are found on the last page of every specially marked "Fashion A Whole New You" Harlequin or Silhouette romance novel). Requests must be received no later than December 31, 1991. Limit: four (4) gifts per name, family, group, organization or address. Items depicted are for illustrative purposes only and may not be exactly as shown. Please allow 6 to 8 weeks for receipt of order. Offer good while quantities of gifts last. In the event an ordered gift is no longer available, you will receive a free, previously unpublished Harlequin or Silhouette book for every proof of purchase you have submitted with your request, plus a refund of the postage and handling charge you have included. Offer good in the U.S. and Canada only.

HQFW-SWPR

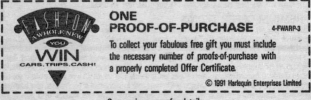